Connectic

LOUISA

Katharine E. Smith

HEDDON PUBLISHING

www.heddonpublishing.com
www.facebook.com/heddonpublishing
@PublishHeddon

 Katharine E. Smith is the author of fifteen novels, including the bestselling Coming Back to Cornwall series. *Louisa* is the third book of the Connections series – also set in Cornwall, but quite different.

A Philosophy graduate, Katharine initially worked in the IT and charity sectors. She turned to freelance editing in 2009, which led to her setting up Heddon Publishing, working with independent authors across the globe.

Katharine lives in Shropshire, UK, with her husband, their two children, and two excitable dogs.

You can find details of her books on her website:
www.katharineesmith.com

Information about her work with other authors can be found here:
www.heddonpublishing.com
and
www.heddonbooks.com

For Dad, John and Rich

LOUISA

Louisa

This is it, then, I guess. The end of London. For now? No, not for now. That's not me. I've made the decision, and there's no going back. Except... now I am going back, in a way.

Ada is delighted, which strengthens my resolve, and makes me smile. Sometimes I feel like I have no idea where I got her from. It doesn't seem wholly out of the question that she was somebody else's baby, and that some other mother, or couple, ended up with a dour, serious, old-before-her-time (like me) daughter, while somehow, I've landed this happy, carefree sun-girl.

"Don't be daft," Mum told me, when I half-joked with her about this. "Lou, you're a strong, strong woman. You've let her grow happy and carefree because you've taken the cares away from her. And anyway, you're not dour, or serious... well, not all of the time."

She had smiled, Mum, but with concern in her eyes. Oh, how she loves me and Laurie, and yet we've both left her miles behind, and forged our own lives. You might think my brother's is the more outlandish choice, currently on a windswept Scottish Isle with mostly just birds for company. But if you could see the life I've lived, and the things I've put myself through to be where I am today, it is quite possible you'd start to change your mind.

I have worked hard. So bloody hard. And now I'm tired. And I know Mum's tired, too. I don't want to leave her anymore. I don't want her to be on her own when she… Let's just say it, Louisa. When she dies. Because she will. There's no point denying it. But I want to be with her now for as long as I can. And I want to tell her all the things I should have told her long ago.

So I wander around the empty house. My empty house. Although, already, it doesn't quite feel like it is mine. It is empty, and clean, and set to be filled with its new owners' things, its new owners' lives. I imagine the excitement and laughter, and small, urgent arguments as decisions are made about what will go where. Voices ringing around the empty rooms, hard edges softening as furniture finds its place and curtains are put up, and this old house transforms into the family's new home.

Still, as my footsteps press across the hard wooden boards of the attic floor (the conversion I paid for and managed, making the most of the available space and maximising the property value – nobody had mentioned what an utter ball-ache that would be), I remember nights gazing out of the window across at the lights of the city; the soft, warm, unfailingly solid shape of my daughter in my arms, pressed to my chest. Ostensibly, I'd be trying to get her back to sleep, but more often than not, I would stay there well after she had closed her eyes and drifted off again.

I can well remember those magical hours, just me and her, and the city before us calm, or as close to calm as it ever could be. I am not one for looking back, nor one for regrets – what's the point? – but I will admit I would give almost anything to travel back to that time, and experience that feeling just once more. I knew then that it was something to be cherished, but I think I had no idea quite how much that was true.

I softly close the doors on the attic, and feel myself wince as I do so. Can I really not go back there? I go down the stairs, saying a silent goodbye to all the rooms now, surprising myself with a *thank you* to each in turn, before shutting them up behind me and turning my back on them one last time. Down the stairs to the hallway, sneaking a final look at the carefully, tastefully renovated living room, and the expensive kitchen, and the garden... my garden. My sacred space. It's time to say goodbye.

1959

Louisa squealed with glee as her dad swung her up and over his head, landing her squarely on his shoulders. Passers-by shot smiles and admiring glances their way. Tall, well-built, and very good-looking, Davey cut an attractive figure, to all the world an adoring, happy-go-lucky dad of a beautiful little girl.

For her part, Louisa was delighted, with her lofty perch and her dad's reassuring, strong hands firmly holding her sturdy legs. Even when he trotted her up and down and she bumped and jiggled into the air ever-so-slightly, she merely giggled, gasping for breath, and grabbing his hair for some extra security.

"Mind out!" Davey exclaimed, though he was smiling. "You'll give me a bald spot!"

Elise and Laurie walked more sedately, some distance behind, Laurie's hand in his mum's, as was usual. 'Mummy's boy', Davey called him or, when he was feeling particularly mean, 'Mummy's girl'. Laurie hated it, and hated him. "Dad was a bastard," he will tell his little sister flatly, one day twelve years or so from now, but that is for the future.

Right now, in this blue-skied moment, when the fishing fleet had returned to town with what felt like a record-breaking catch, and bunting fluttered all along the harbour front, Louisa looked back towards her mum and her brother, and down on the passers-by, and waved like a little queen. She was safe on her daddy's shoulders, and there was not a place in the world that she would rather be.

Louisa

It doesn't take long for my mother and me to be irritated by each other. It's over something so trivial as well.

I've bought one of 'those' flats, you see. The new ones by the harbour. In the Saltings – the development owned and run by Canyon Holdings, an American company who I have been working with over the last couple of years. No, I didn't get a discount on my apartment, unfortunately. I did have second thoughts about my choice of home – not so much because of the local disapproval but because it's meant handing over my hard-earned money – and a lot of it – to a company which has not treated me particularly well. Although, if I am being honest, it was my own employer who really let me down. After all the years and hours I've put in for them, regularly putting my own (and sometimes Ada's) needs aside, when it came to the crunch they didn't hesitate to let me go, to save face, and save the lucrative contract with Canyon.

Still, this is really the best place for me around here. I couldn't live in a little terraced house like Mum's, and I don't want one of the big town houses further up the hill. I had my big house in London. It's time for something smaller and low-maintenance. The flat is both these things, and has the added bonus of never having been lived in before, by anyone. There are no layers of dust from previous residents, as in my London house, where Ada and I have now added our own contribution. No backstory to speak of. No ghosts (unless you count the lone fisherman who is said to haunt the harbour, but I'm two floors up here so I'm not too worried). Somehow, in my absence, my once understated but always beautiful home county (*Duchy*, I hear myself being sternly corrected by Mum's friend Bill – in fact, more than a few people believe Cornwall is a country in its own right) has increased a hundred-fold in popularity, and become the place to be, or the place to buy a second home. Maybe a third; a fourth; a fifth... you get the picture...

House prices and holiday prices have become inflated beyond belief. It's possible that could fall apart at some point. But this flat will hold its value, should I ever wish to sell.

You might think Mum would object to the Saltings, like many of the other locals do, but she's not like that. "Change has got to come," she will say, "for better or for worse." So it isn't my choice of flat that's the problem. Rather, it's my refusal to let her help me clean it.

"I'm elderly, not an invalid," she huffs at me.

"I realise that, Mum." But I stick to my guns and tell her I'll be fine doing it myself. She might think it's because I didn't want her tiring herself out or something. Somehow, I can't bring myself to tell her the real reason. I just want to do this on my own. Like I've done everything else in my life, since I left home, and left Cornwall for good (as I thought I was doing back then).

After Dad died, I was very clingy. I hid in Mum's shadow. John, my therapist, suggests that is quite normal for a child who has lost a parent. The natural reaction is to worry that your other parent might die, too. Elise Morgan (she changed her surname back to her maiden name after Dad died, and changed mine and Laurie's, too) is not an overbearing type – quite the opposite. She made me feel safe, but when I look back I must never have felt truly safe, because I had seen that bad things happen. Not just in books or TV shows. People actually die, in real life (or death). I had stayed close to my mum at all times, and Laurie had been the same. But something had turned in me when I was a teenager. I remember one of my friends, Marian, telling me that I'd be just like my mum when I grew up, and my reaction shocked both of us.

"No I won't!" I exploded. "I'm nothing like her."

"OK," Marian had said, "but it was meant as a compliment. I wish my mum was more like yours."

"Yeah, well, you don't know her," I'd blustered. It was shortly after Laurie, my brother, had told me a bit about our dad, you see. He could remember Davey Plummer. I couldn't, although I often pretended I could. And back then, my slightly skewed take on reality somehow had me apportioning some blame to my mum – when I know now of course that any culpability sits squarely on my dad's shoulders.

Laurie's revelations had the effect of sending me off in a very different direction to what I'd imagined for my life. I was unsettled, not just by what he said, but by realising Mum didn't share everything with me in the way I'd thought she did. I always felt like I was closer to her than Laurie was; that she and I had a special bond. Realising that she had kept from me something so very vital about our lives made me question this. Of course, with much hindsight and a more grown-up, mother's perspective, I can rationalise it. Understand it. But that slight had buried itself deep within me, and I still can't quite shake it off. I still won't accept her help. I am far too used to my stubborn independence by now.

Still, Mum is a little bit hurt, and a little bit annoyed. But she is also a realist, and she knows me, and she will bounce back. She always does.

To move things on, I offer to take her out for dinner.

"I could do us some tea," Mum says, as I had known she would.

I bite back my exasperation. Why can't she just accept my offer?

"I know, Mum, thank you. And that would be really nice. But let's go out tonight. Let's celebrate!"

I am sure she thinks I'm a terrible spendthrift. A flashy London type, coming down and throwing all my money around. It's not that, though. I really do want to treat her, and I do want to celebrate. And I also love the way she is when we're at Tregynon – the hotel and restaurant that was previously a manor house, where Mum spent such intense, diverse times. First as a schoolgirl during the war, when her all-girls' school was evacuated to Cornwall from Surrey, and then as a governess. Her mum had died during the war and her dad a long time before that.

When Mum finished her schooling, she had nowhere to go. Nowhere to return to. So she stayed in Cornwall, and taught the children of the family who had come back to their ancestral home – complete with extensive gardens and private beach. It all seems such a world away, and utterly outlandish compared to my own fairly ordinary childhood, and my working life. And, while I know she must have had some difficult times at Tregynon, being there never fails to bring a sparkle to her eyes, and a lovely, gentle flush to her cheeks.

And yet, I can't just tell her this, although I really should. If not now, then when? But there's that block, isn't there? The one therapist John has always banged on about. Something so deep-rooted in the past, it sits between me and Mum and I can't seem to break through it. I can't quite get through to her.

John is something else I can't tell her about. I've been seeing him for years. Very American, she'd say – like she said about AJ.

"Alright then," Mum says, and all of a sudden, she sounds brighter. "You're absolutely right, my girl, this is something to celebrate. You've come back! What could possibly be better than that?"

Of course, Mum insists on walking up the steep hill to the hotel, despite the fact I would have happily driven.

"Louisa, the day I stop walking is the day I stop. Full stop." She chuckles.

"OK," I smile, and actually I'm glad. It's a beautiful evening for a walk, and it also means I can have a couple of glasses of wine. Another habit I'll try to break now I'm here. But there is something about that satisfying pop of a cork set free from the bottle. The first sip of crisp, chilled white, at the end of a long day. Maybe I won't be as drawn to it now that I don't have a job. What a very odd thought.

The light of the evening seeps into me, as I walk with my mum up and out of town, and with it comes a lightness of step. I breathe in slowly and my eyes take it all in – sights at once so familiar, and yet somehow so new. I can make out the fishing fleet returning to shore, now expected to mingle with a few extravagant pleasure craft which seem to me to have strayed from elsewhere. They move pluckily across the depths of the sea, its changing colours and dangerous rips.

As we walk, we disturb the tiny songbirds, which flit around the tangled hedgerow guarding the untouched patch of wilderness between the road and the cliffs, tracking our progress.

The sun, for the most part hidden by soft puffs of cloud, still manages to make the sea sparkle. A final, magical gift for the day before it vanishes beyond the horizon and darkness sets in.

What would I be doing now, if I was back home? In my old home, I mean. In London. At this time of night, I might have been still in the office, or on a crowded train – or in my kitchen, perched at the breakfast bar with a glass in hand, an uncorked bottle on the counter, and my laptop casting an unnatural glow onto my face. How many nights over the years have I spent like that? Too many, multiplied by ten. It may take a while to decompress from the intense life I've led, but perhaps it will take less time than I'd imagined.

Mum keeps pace with me as we walk, and in fact it's me that wants to slow down. I would like to stop and savour the place, the view, the smells – but I don't, for fear she will think I'm doing it for her benefit. She's a proud woman, my mother. Perhaps she and I are not so different after all.

"I still can't really believe you're here," Mum says, her eyes shining.

We are seated at a table for two by one of the huge windows, and have a view across the grounds, towards the woods that bank steeply down to the little beach. A pair of blackbirds hop across the grass, while a gull struts regally along the balustrade at the edge of the expansive patio.

"It's only a month or two since I was last here. And we ate at that table right over there!" I pretend not to understand her meaning. But she's not stupid and she knows that neither am I.

"You know what I mean, Lou. I can't believe you've come back. I honestly didn't think I'd see the day."

"Well, it just seemed like time for a change. I'm not getting any younger–" Mum has a wry laugh at this, no doubt thinking she has twenty-odd years on me – "honestly, Mum, some of the people I'm sitting round the table with were born in the 1980s! Actually, I'll be honest – the 1990s!"

She laughs again, as I had hoped she would. This time a full, honest laugh. But she knows there is more to it than this. There is AJ. Somebody I was in a relationship with and am now not. She does not push for an explanation, but I know she must be wondering what went wrong.

I never tell Mum about my romantic dalliances – not that there are so many of them. But with him, I had allowed myself to hope, and I wanted her to know. I had let my guard down. I must be getting soft in my old age.

I am grateful that she is not the type to press too hard for details. I truly believe, without wishing to sound arrogant, or to overstate my importance to her life, that right now she is just happy I've come back to roost.

"You could run circles round those youngsters," she says.

"Maybe, maybe not. I might have lost whatever it is I had. But also, I just don't think I want to anymore. I am starting to think there may be more to life."

"Oh, my love. I hope you find it here. I hope you don't get bored. It's going to be very strange for you, not working. And living somewhere so small. So quiet. It could take some time to acclimatise."

"I know. I do know that. And I've decided I'm not going to stop work altogether. But I am going to do things differently. Maybe some volunteer work. I thought I might ask Maggie, actually, if she knows of anything…"

"That is a wonderful idea!" Mum exclaims. "She'll definitely know what's going on. I can give you her number."

She is eager for her new friend Maggie – who is far younger than either of us – and me to connect, but it will take more than this.

Dinner is delicious. I have lobster, while Mum chooses roasted aubergine linguine. This is the influence of Maggie and her daughter, Stevie – both committed vegetarians – but I don't mind in the way that Mum thinks I do. In fact, I don't really mind at all. It is more that I envy the easy relationship that Mum and Maggie seem to share, when my own relationship with Mum can be so stilted.

I remind myself that if Maggie was closer to Mum's age, I wouldn't be having these thoughts at all. I would just be glad that Mum had found a new friend. I know how much she has struggled since her best friend Maudie died. I also know that it must be perfectly normal to have friction between mums and daughters...

I see Mum's eyes on me. There are questions there, but I am not ready to answer them. Still, she can see that I'm not quite there with her. I give myself a little inward mental shake, and try to push all of these thoughts aside. Therapist John tells me I am too inward-looking, and it's because I spend too much time on my own. He is right, of course, but is it any wonder?

"I had a lovely message from Ada today," Mum says, smiling, and I know she has got us onto safe ground. We are united always in our love and admiration of Ada, and Mum knows this.

"Oh yes?" I say. "Did she have any news?"

"She says she's settling in and has some nice flatmates. She sounds excited about starting her course as well."

"Oh, I know. I'm so jealous. I wish I was starting out all over again. Do you ever wish you'd gone to university?"

"Maybe," she says. "But it wasn't going to happen for me. I'm just so glad you and Laurie were able to go."

And that is it in a nutshell. Motherhood. Being genuinely happier that your children got to do something you didn't. There will never be anyone on this earth who loves me in the way that my mum loves me. I need to acknowledge that fact, and to cherish it.

While we wait for our food, and sip our drinks, I tell Mum tales she has not heard before, from my student days, and I'm gratified by her laughter.

Tregynon is a beautiful place to sit and eat. It's seen so many changes over the last decades. The extravagant dining room must have been wasted on those Whiteleys schoolgirls, although from what Mum says, some of them would have come from this kind of house themselves – and I don't mean they'd have been on the staff.

Poor clever Mum, with her scholarship. She could have run rings around them all, as she is suggesting I could do with my young, talented colleagues, but would she have? I suspect not. It's not just about intelligence and talent. It's confidence. It's feeling like you belong. And those types – bred with money and entitlement – often exude it. They have no doubt that they are in the right place. The scholarship girls, meanwhile, doubt everything. Imposter syndrome.

I sent Ada to our local state schools back in London, which I know surprised some people, but I wanted her to be easy with everyone, and never to expect privilege. Although I will admit that this was hard to accomplish, given that she had a childminder when she was at primary school, and a beautiful big house, and piano lessons... expensive holidays. Despite all of that, she has managed to keep her feet on the ground. I may be proud of my career and everything I have achieved at work, but Ada is my greatest accomplishment by far. I don't think I can really take credit for her, though.

I've ordered an expensive wine (I can't tell Mum how expensive) and a couple of glasses in, it's going to my head. Maybe it's an after-effect of all the delicious sea air as well. It feels good, and I am beginning to relax.

Mum, of course, knows the names of everyone who works at Tregynon. It means I can sit back and just unwind, while she chats with various members of staff, asking after people's partners, parents, children... she is clearly well known, and well liked, around here. I find myself envying her.

She also knows this place inside-out. I like to watch the expressions that cross her face when she's looking around, not realising my eyes are on her. I think of her as a little girl; try to imagine what it must have been like, arriving here in a gaggle of schoolmates and teachers, while the war was raging away. When I was very young, I found the idea of the war exciting. The sound of air raid sirens at once terrifying and thrilling. The reality, I'm sure, would have been just terrifying. And at the same time I imagine it may well have become boring, and depressing, with depleted food supplies, and enforced blackouts. It was also no doubt very lonely, perhaps especially for children sent away from their families. For their own safety, yes, but what would that do to a child, to be separated in such a way? At such a time.

Once I had Ada, I knew there was no way I could bear to be parted from her. Which may sound odd, given that it didn't take long for me to get back to work, and I employed a nanny to take care of her day-to-day. But I had to keep my job. I couldn't let all of that slip away. Yet all day long, I would look forward to returning home. No matter what the time of night, I would sneak into her room if she was asleep, and I'd just sit there and watch her little chest rising and falling, finding my own breath synchronising with hers. Whenever I could, I would be home in time to do her bath and bed, knowing that an empty evening would then stretch ahead and provide all the opportunity I needed to catch up with work.

"Did you mind coming here? To Cornwall, I mean." I realise I've never really asked her before. She looks surprised at the question.

"With Whiteleys?" she asks, for clarification. "Or the Camelford-Bassetts?"

"Well, with Whiteleys, I suppose. Though I would love to know what it was like working for that family!"

"Ha!" Mum smiles. "I must have told you about all that!"

"No, Mum." She knows full well she hasn't. "Just the basics."

"Well, there is a bit of a story, I suppose..." Her eyes have taken on a twinkle.

"Oh really?"

Mum takes a sip of her wine, regarding me across the top of her glass. And then she begins to colour in a little more of her early life for me – years which had in my mind been two-dimensional and fairly dull. A necessary existence, but just an existence, I'd thought. Never imagining that she'd been close to an affair with the lord of the manor. That saying, about the apple falling close to the tree, springs to mind.

"He didn't!" I can't help exclaiming, when she describes how Lord Camelford-Bassett had kissed her one night, when they were out in the garden of Lanhydrock House. "I can't believe you've never told me this before!"

"I know," she muses. "I suppose, when you left home, I thought you didn't need to know about that. But I tried to warn you, in my way. About men. You know... taking advantage."

She did. I remember the lectures, as I had thought of

them then. I remember not wanting to hear them.

"I bet Grandma would have hated you being used as a lady's maid, too."

I like to call her Grandma – Annabel, who I never met, and yet feel such a connection to. Born in the early twentieth century, she lived through the first world war, but the second one got her. She was a nurse. A single mother (although she had been married for a brief time, until my grandad died) – the first in a line of mothers who have raised their children single-handedly.

"Yes, I think she probably would have. Angela Forbes used to say that to me. Angela knew about his lordship, too. She saw that coming way before I did. Do you know," Mum leans in conspiratorially, and I consider that the wine has maybe gone to her head as well, "Angela and my mum were close."

"Close?"

"Yes, as in... more than friends."

I feel my eyebrows shoot up. "They were?"

"Yes, or at least I think so. I didn't see it while Mum was alive; I don't suppose I even realised that was a thing back then. I was really quite green as a girl. But Davey – your dad – he knew. I don't know how. He wasn't nice about it. A lot of people couldn't accept those kind of relationships back then."

"A lot of people still can't."

"In time, I pieced it together. And I could see it then."

"Does it bother you?"

"No. Why should it? What does bother me is that they never got to enjoy it. They never got to be open about it, or spend more than a few days together. But I suppose in those years there was many a relationship spoiled, for

17

lots of different reasons. People had to live away from those they loved. And so many lives were lost. There were so many widows and orphans. It was just how it was. But no, if you mean do I mind that they loved each other, I don't mind at all. Angela was like another parent to me. Because she loved my mum."

"And because she loved you."

"Well, yes, she did. But that only came about because of Mum."

I look at my own mother, with tears in my eyes. This woman, once a little girl with no dad, and then no mum, reliant on her teacher to take her in and set her off on the right path. What if there had been no Angela? What then? But that is a futile train of thought. Life has happened as it has happened. What's the point in going back and trying to imagine it being any different?

"She would have loved you," Mum said, putting her hand on mine. "And Laurie, of course. But yes, your grandma would have loved you."

We're lucky to get a lift back down to town with Rob, one of the bar staff from Tregynon. He's mum's friend Bill's nephew/grandson/cousin twice removed. Something like that. He's very kind and chatty, and he drops Mum at her door. I get out with her.

"Would you like a coffee?" she asks me.

"I won't, thanks, Mum." I see the disappointment flash across her face, although she does her best to hide it. "But I'd love a cup of tea," I say, and she smiles. It's going to take some getting used to, having to consider Mum on a regular basis. I see now how I've barely given a thought to her over the years. The odd cursory visit here and there, more often than not staying at a hotel or a rental place. While I'd told myself that was out of consideration for her, and a way to ensure I could work uninterrupted if I needed to, this was really only partly true. I hadn't wanted to be cooped up in my old room, and I hadn't wanted Mum and me to be on top of each other. I have always wanted to do things my way. Even to the point of having what I want for breakfast, when I want it. I'm a snob, I know. I wasn't always, but I've grown used to things a certain way. My way.

It won't hurt to come in for half an hour, and as I follow Mum into the small, familiar hallway and comfortable, peaceful lounge, I am glad to be here.

For a long time, I couldn't think of anything worse than coming home. Now, I'm starting to believe that there can't be anything better.

1959

"Where is Daddy? Where is he?"

"Shut *up*, Louisa. Shut *up*," Laurie miserably instructed his little sister through gritted teeth. He knew. Their dad was dead. And he hadn't liked his dad, but he had desperately wanted his dad to like him. And he had sometimes thought he wished Davey would go away, but now he knew what that meant. He'd thought that maybe if their dad went away, their mum would be happy, but she wasn't.

Bobby Latham at school had no dad – he had died when the fishing boat he worked on had sunk, and everyone said what a hero he was, because he had managed to save his friend's life, but lost his own in the process. Sometimes, Laurie had wished that it was his dad who had died. And now he had. It was all his fault.

"I want Daddy!" Louisa launched into a full-blown toddler tantrum and Laurie put his hands over his ears, hunching himself up on the chair. Not Davey's chair. Even now he was gone, nobody sat there. Laurie wanted to push it into the fire, but he knew that was not a good idea.

Elise, meanwhile – their mum – just pulled Louisa onto her knee and shushed her. Rocking her absentmindedly, her eyes gazing towards something that Laurie could not see.

"Mummy?" he tried tentatively. "Mum?"

She didn't answer. Did she know it was because of him? Was that why she couldn't look at him? But no—

"Shall we have boiled eggs for tea, Laurie?" She turned to him now with a smile and he felt much better.

"Yes, please," he said as solemnly and as politely as he

could, wanting to keep her smiling.

She stood, pulling Louisa onto her hip. "Come on, then," she ruffled his hair. "Let's go and see what the girls have for us, shall we?"

The 'girls' were the hens who belonged to their neighbour, Marie, who had invited Laurie to come over and see if they had laid any eggs during the day. "You see, Laurie, there'll be three, just enough for you and your mum and your sister."

And she was right! Laurie did find three eggs, just as Marie had promised. They were still warm, and it felt ever so slightly like stealing, taking the hens' treasure that they had carefully hidden in the hay.

Elise assured him that the eggs were not ever going to be baby chickens, as Marie only had hens. "They meant them for us," she said. "Didn't Marie tell you they would?"

She had put Louisa down, and the little girl was walking unsteadily across Marie's garden. Then there she was, their neighbour, her arms held out to the little girl, and a huge smile on her face.

Louisa ran to her, and the woman scooped her up into a cuddle. "I'm going to miss you!" she exclaimed, pressing her cheek – dry and worn from a lifetime living high above the sea – against the little girl's, which was soft and warm, and felt like innocence itself.

"We'll miss you too," Elise told Marie. "Come and visit, won't you? We're only down the hill."

Because Louisa and Laurie and Elise were moving. To Angela's house. Angela, their friend and the headmistress at the school, who had also died. Not long before their dad had. It had Laurie's head in a whirl, all this death. Sometimes he had to just shut his eyes, and hope that it would all go away, but sometimes that only made him feel worse.

"I will, of course. But you'll be busy with that job of yours, and your little-uns. Don't be afraid to ask for help."

Marie had put her arm around Elise's shoulder. She handed Louisa over. Laurie was looking up at the three of them and feeling a little bit lost. But Louisa kicked against her mum, to be put down, and she put her solid little arms around her brother, like she knew that was exactly what he needed.

"Thank you for the eggs, Marie," Laurie said shyly, at Elise's prompting.

"It's my pleasure, little-un." Marie took Laurie by the shoulders and then swept him into a hug. "You take care of your mum and your little sister, okay? You're the man of the house now."

"We'll all take care of each other," Elise said firmly, although not rudely. She didn't want Laurie feeling any more weight than he already did, on his little shoulders.

She had folded the eggs into the hem of her cardigan, and wrapped it around them to keep them safe. Laurie took Louisa's hand, and they followed their mum home for one last night in the cottage on the cliffs.

Louisa

"Oh, hi Louisa!" Maggie sounds surprised, and I can't work out if she is pleased or not. Never mind, I've made the call, and now I need to push on. I didn't get where I am – where I was – by being bashful.

"How are you, Maggie?" I am using my work voice, I can hear it, and I feel powerless to stop it. Brusque and no-nonsense. That's me.

"I'm fine, thanks... yes, fine..." She sounds doubtful, and I don't know if that's just her way. Is she always a bit flaky? Or is there something on her mind?

"Good, good. Well, I do hope Mum told you she'd given me your number."

"She did, yes, that's absolutely fine."

"Super." *Super?* When do I ever say *super*? "Well, she might also have told you I'm looking for some work. Possibly voluntary work. I need to keep busy! And I've got lots of skills that I'd like to put to good use. I wonder if you know of anything?"

"I'm sure there's loads of places that could do with some help," she says, "but I know you need to find the right one for you. I was volunteering at the seniors' club at first when I moved here. You know... Caring the Community," she says, with a note of apology in her voice, as though she named the thing herself.

"Ah yes! Mum hates that name," I allow myself a chuckle.

"She certainly does. God knows who came up with it. Anyway, I know they're looking for somebody else... but I'm guessing that's not for you?"

"God, no! No offence."

"None taken! I have a feeling that you might be better suited to one of the bigger concerns, maybe the food hub? It's run by a woman called Judith... Jude, I think. She's very good, but she's always saying she hasn't got enough time – she wants to broaden what they offer, so they can support new parents who are struggling. Help people who can't afford their heating bills. That kind of thing."

"OK..." I say, thinking. "That could be interesting. Do you know how I might get in touch?"

"Well, they're in tomorrow, at the Saltings, I mean. They've got a base outside town, but they use our community space every week to set up the Pantry, as they call it – so people can easily come and pick up some things, and get some advice as well if they need it. It's great, actually."

"Fantastic. I might just drop in and say hello. Thank you, Maggie."

"No problem."

"Say hi to Tony for me." I can't help myself. Reminding her that her new boyfriend and I have some kind of history. I hang up before she can answer.

I have a leisurely breakfast in my new flat. I had actually woken up at 5.30 (old habits die hard), my mind whizzing, but I'd made a cup of tea, brought it back to bed, and switched on Radio 4. Sinking back against the cushions, I practised alternate-nostril-breathing the way John had taught me as a way to unwind, and I woke up for a second time this morning at nearly quarter to eight, a cold cup of tea on the bedside table, and seagulls making a racket from the roof. It may be quieter here than in London, but I'm going to have to reacquaint myself with all these different sounds. I might even miss the white noise of the traffic; even the sirens. There's something comforting in knowing life is going on outside, even in the wee small hours.

From my dining table, I have a view of the harbour, via the glass doors which lead onto the tiny balcony. It's quite something, seeing the place where I grew up from this vantage point. I must be nearly on a level with Tregynon, and out of sight from here, on the other side of town, is the little cottage where I once lived with my mum and dad and brother. Until my dad died, and it was just me and my mum and my brother. And then we moved into Angela's house on Godolphin Terrace, where Mum still lives now.

Sometimes I think Mum would be better accepting one of the offers she says she regularly receives, from companies wanting to buy her house as a holiday-let. I can see it would do well with holiday-makers, being ideally situated across from the beach and close to the railway station. No parking, of course, but then that's the case with most of the properties central to the town. This place was not built for traffic.

Mum won't hear of it, though. If she gets her way, she'll be there till her dying day, and I hope that is not for quite some time.

"You're not to sell it on though, Lou, you hear? When I'm gone, I mean. It's for you and Laurie and Ada. And if none of you want to live here, you can rent it to a local person or a family. OK?"

"OK." I've heard these instructions many times. I know Mum would never make this legally binding, but I doubt that any of us would want to go against her wishes.

This is a morbid train of thought, though – my mum's death. The way I've lived the last forty years, there's a good chance I could be gone before her anyway. Laurie is much more wholesome. He'll probably get his 100th birthday telegram.

After my granola and yoghurt, and a second cup of coffee, I shower and dress in what I hope are casual-enough clothes. A pair of expensive jeans, a plaid shirt, and some black mid-calf boots. I will need to update my wardrobe for life in Cornwall, although I wouldn't be seen dead in the type of baggy, saggy clothes Maggie wears. Hoodies and t-shirts at her age!

Stop, I tell myself. *You're not meant to be bothered by her.* I am, though, a little. We are similar in height, and build, and have very similar hair and colouring, but she is young enough to be my daughter. And she has Tony, while I have no-one. I hate the way I keep comparing myself to her, and I'm not proud of the fact that I'm glad I have more money, and better clothes, than her.

I push open the door of the Saltings community space, which bears a notice proclaiming: 'Welcome to the Pantry'. I see a room full of people. There are shelves of supermarket-type crates lining the edges of the room, with an orderly queue of people making their way around, with shopping baskets. In the centre of the room are two desks, with people sitting either side. A woman of indeterminate age comes towards me. She has short, greying hair, and a nose-ring. She is dressed in baggy tie-dye trousers and a kind of woven hoodie. She has very intense blue eyes.

"Can I help you?" she asks, smiling.

"I'm… yes, but I don't need anything," I say, all tense at the thought she might consider me somebody who needs her charity.

"Oh?" she asks, still smiling.

"No, I've come to see if I can help, actually." I know the exact look I have on my face. Like I've never cracked a smile in my life. It's a front, a defence built up over the years, but I don't suppose I look very approachable.

Nevertheless, the woman carries on smiling. "That's wonderful! We're always on the lookout for new volunteers. Would you be able to come to an interview?"

"An interview?" I'd assumed they'd be grateful for any help they could get.

"Yes. And I'll need you to fill out a form. And complete a DBS check, if you don't mind. That is, if we find we want to work together. I'm Jude, by the way."

She holds out her hand. I take it. "Louisa."

"Nice to meet you, Louisa. If you'd like to go and see Tamsin over there, she can take your contact details and we'll get some bumf over to you."

Bumf? I think. That's not even a real word. Is it? Still, I suppose it suggests this is a well-organised outfit, so really I should approve.

Tamsin is slender and willowy, with short, bleached hair and a bright smile. I wait my turn, watching her speak to the people sitting at the desk before her. Two women –

perhaps a mother and daughter – the younger one clearly trying to hold back tears. Tamsin is kind and patient with them, writing down a few notes before directing them to a bearded man near the boxes of groceries.

She looks up, and I notice she does a very quick, scarcely visible, once-over of me. She, I think, can see that my clothes are expensive – I suspect Jude would not have had an inkling.

"Can I help you?" Tamsin asks smoothly.

"Oh, yes, thank you. Jude said to come and see you. I'd like to offer my services, if I can. I've just moved here, you see."

"Oh, you won't regret it. It's the best place in the world!"

"I'm moving back, actually," I correct myself, and her. "I was born here, went to the little school up the hill." Is it my imagination, or am I encouraging a slight Cornish lilt into my voice?

"Really?" she smiles more widely. "That's even better. I've nothing against the incomers, you know, not like a lot of people round here. But it's nicer to have people moving back. You already know what it's like, don't you? Not expecting it to be all cream teas and fudge!"

"Definitely not," I say, and I look meaningfully around the room. "Unless those boxes are just full of fudge, clotted cream and pasties?"

Tamsin laughs. "I don't think so!"

Somehow, I feel more at ease with her than with Jude. I think perhaps she's a bit more urban. Less Guardian-reading liberal.

"Right, let me get your name and email address, and I'll send you some info and a form. Then we'll get you in to the HQ for a chat."

"Smashing," I smile. "Thanks."

She takes down my details, and I move along, realising I am taking up valuable consultation time. I am shocked at the number of people in here. I knew that there was a need for food banks, of course, but this is a small town, yet there seem to be a lot of people in this room.

As I walk out, I resolve to do what I can to help. *These are my people, after all*, I think, then I smile. What do I sound like? Like one of the people Tamsin alluded to, who don't want people moving in. Incomers. *Strangers.* I can see both sides of the coin, and I'm aware that I didn't want to tell Tamsin where I live. That I may be from round here, but I'm also one of those who have bought into the evil Saltings. My god, I even helped this development to happen in the first place. Still, I'll have to put my details on the application form, so she'll know soon enough.

I check my watch. 10.45am. What now? The rest of the day yawns emptily ahead of me. This is going to take some getting used to. I have itchy feet, and I know I'm going to feel irritable soon if I don't do something constructive. But what? I suppose I could find out what else is going on locally.

The smell of coffee wanders into my nostrils, so I decide to pop into the little café on the ground floor – my third cup of coffee already, I'll be jittery soon – even though I could just as easily return to my apartment and make myself a drink. I feel like, well, not company, exactly, but noise. Chatter. As though I am not completely alone, with nothing to do.

1971

Growing up, Louisa was glad that they were in town, although Laurie often lamented not having that lofty view of the sea that they had from the cottage and its garden. He missed being able to easily watch the comings and goings of the birds and other sea life. Sometimes it was possible to see a gleaming pod of dolphins arching their way up and down across the waves. There had even been rumours of a whale, although Laurie had not seen it himself.

For Louisa, though, town was where it was at – until it too came to feel too small. As a youngster, she felt like the quiet, narrow terraces, the beaches and harbour, were all she would ever need. Her friends lived in the maze of streets and they could, and often did, easily meet each other. Louisa was lucky that her mum was always happy for her friends to be around at their house, so if the weather was bad or when the winter nights closed in early, it didn't curtail Louisa's social life.

She didn't have a best friend, as some of the girls did, but she was never short of company. It pained her a little that her brother was more of a loner, and she felt ashamed that she had to actively fight a feeling of embarrassment about him. He wasn't bothered about his appearance, or about girls, or even about boys. He liked birds, and animals, and walking the coastal paths. It was just who he was, she knew, and if she ever forgot, their mum would be quick to remind her.

"He's not like you and me," Elise would tell her daughter. "He finds friendships... difficult."

Louisa wasn't convinced that their mum was right

about that. She thought Laurie just wasn't particularly interested in friendships, full stop. He was a kind, funny and caring big brother to her – and he was friendly enough to her friends. She even thought Susan might have a crush on him. Not that Laurie would notice. It seemed to Louisa that her brother could easily have a big group of friends if he wanted to. He could even have a girlfriend, if he could be bothered with his clothes, and made an effort to tame his unruly hair. He was a good-looking boy. She could see it when she looked closely at him, but it was almost like he made every effort to hide that about himself.

Still, she was pleased at the way her mum likened herself to Louisa. 'Not like you and me'. They were alike – everyone said it – not in looks, but in temperament.

"You're strong, like your mum," Elise's best friend, Maudie, would often tell Louisa. "I thought they'd broken the mould when they made her, but then along you came."

Louisa loved being with her mum and Maudie. There was something conspiratorial about being among women, and she would often choose to walk along with them if they went to the beach with Laurie and Maudie's husband, Fred. She liked to hear her mum's conversations with Maudie, and be included in the confidences which passed between them, although it felt frustratingly like they held back sometimes.

Whenever her mum and Maudie allowed Louisa access to their conversations, she cherished each revelation as though they had dropped a precious jewel into her hands. Laurie was not privy to them – not that he would care either way – and it made Louisa feel very grown-up, and trusted. She knew that Maudie and Fred had wanted to have children but couldn't, and that made Maudie sad. She also knew that Fred's sister Gladys was considering breaking up from her husband, who kept cheating on her with the barmaid from their local pub. That Sylvia Gladstone was having *another* baby (number six!) and that the vicar's wife was a terrible gossip, and not to be trusted. They never really talked about Elise, though, and Louisa supposed it was because there wasn't anything to say. She was a widow and a mum of two. She worked at a law office in town, and she didn't have any siblings or parents, and her best friends were Maudie and Fred, who they saw all the time, and with whom Elise never fell out.

What could there possibly be to talk about?

On quiet Sunday afternoons, when friends were with their extended families or on Sunday-school outings, Laurie would often be out on one of his wildlife-watching excursions and so Louisa and Elise would have the house to themselves. More often than not, they could be found either end of the window seat, each lost in a book. Elise favoured writers like Daphne du Maurier, and D.H. Lawrence and George Eliot, while Louisa was more interested in modern authors, who fired her imagination and broadened her world view – although she was not actively aware this was what she was doing. She had been reading a book called *To Kill a Mockingbird*, which had introduced her to the concept of the life and treatments of African Americans. It was so far removed from Cornwall, where there were next to no black people, although she had heard of black GIs being posted here during the war. Despite the clear issues this book highlighted, it lent America a sheen of mystery and other-worldiness, which Louisa thought she would like to experience.

Her mum was from London – a fact she was very proud of. When the majority of her classmates were born and bred in the town where they lived – as were their parents and grandparents before them – Louisa clung on to this fact that her background was quite different, and exotic, her own mum having come from the capital city, which none of her friends had ever visited. Neither had Louisa, but she didn't feel the need to clarify that, instead casting herself as the expert on all things London.

She would go one day, though. Her mum kept saying so, but Laurie really didn't want to go.

"It's too noisy," he'd say. "Too busy."

"Well I guess it'll be just you and me then, Lou," Elise would smile at Louisa, giving her that glow of inclusion. "When I've saved up enough, we'll go for a weekend, shall we?"

And they had. And it had been fantastic. Louisa had looked forward to it for weeks, since the time that her mum had set the dates and made sure that Maudie and Fred were happy to keep an eye on Laurie (who was adamant he was old enough to stay at home alone, and more than sensible enough to mean Elise had no concerns about his safety, or him inviting unsavoury friends around – as already established, Laurie didn't have any particular friends anyway, unsavoury or otherwise).

They had taken the train across to St Erth, and Louisa had gazed out across the estuary, trying to see what it was that held so much magic to Laurie. She just couldn't. It was flat, and grey, and so very quiet. It was boring.

They changed onto a bigger train at St Erth, and even that was enough to provoke a sense of excitement. There were new people – different people – boarding alongside them, all aboard the Cornish Riviera Express.

"Cornish Riviera!" Elise said, grinning at Louisa.

"What?"

"Well... it's clever marketing, isn't it? Mind you, Cornwall is somewhere special. We'll have to watch out or in fifty years we'll be over-run by holiday-makers!"

"I doubt it, Mum. It's Cornwall, isn't it? Boring."

"You'll appreciate it one day."

Louisa didn't respond. She was too busy taking in the sight of the other passengers. There were four young women, maybe only five years older than her, seated at a table a couple of rows in front, all chatting excitedly. Then a couple, maybe in their twenties, the man pushing a case up onto the luggage rack before sitting heavily back down and putting his arm around the woman, who rested her head smilingly against his shoulder. He planted a kiss on her head. The woman spotted Louisa looking and she smiled at the girl, which made Louisa look hurriedly away.

As the train rattled along and dug into the journey, Louisa sent an occasional glance at the couple and noted that the woman seemed to have dozed off, while the man had removed his arm from around her shoulder (it must have ached after a while, thought Louisa) and become engrossed in a book.

Elise, too, was reading, and Louisa was holding her own book, but she couldn't settle into it.

In time, Elise produced some paper-wrapped sandwiches, made from thick slices of a home-made loaf. Louisa bit thankfully into hers, her mouth watering at the butter, cheese and pickle. She hadn't realised how hungry she was. Elise had also packed bottles of ginger beer, and some apples. Louisa polished hers off, and then sat back to watch the countryside and towns roll past. She found her eyes beginning to shut, and her own head lolling against her mother's shoulder.

Every now and then, the train would stop, and she would hear announcements about the station they were pausing in, and a reminder of the final destination of the train. The thought of London created a delicious anticipation in her half-waking mind, but she knew it was the last stop, and not one they could miss. She felt Elise's head against her own, and she kept her eyes closed, relishing the feeling of it being just the two of them, heading out into the world while the train wheels rattled and rolled beneath them.

Louisa

"Hello?" there is a tentative voice from behind my right shoulder. I've taken a high seat at one of the tables against the café window. It means I can watch the comings and goings of the harbour, and also have my back to the room – which in theory should mean that I don't have to interact with anyone. But clearly this person thinks otherwise.

I turn to see a vaguely familiar, very glamorous, woman... maybe late thirties or early forties.

"Hello," I say, with what I hope is just the right amount of disinterest. Over the years at work, I've honed my voice and my mannerisms to convey that I am busy, that I am not particularly approachable, but that I am also not 100% unfriendly. It seems that all of this goes over the woman's head, as she hops onto the seat next to me, like a bird, perching on the edge.

"I'm Stacey?" she thrusts out her hand. "Your neighbour?" She has a rising inflection at the end of each statement. Something that has always annoyed me, but I've had to get used to, since Ada and her friends all speak like this. This woman has a distinctly Northern accent too. I find it hard to distinguish Yorkshire from Lancashire, though. I don't suppose it really matters, aside from to people from one or other of those places.

"Ah, yes." That's where I've seen her before. She's got the maisonette. She also has three boys, and a husband, or partner. They're quite noisy.

She looks at me expectantly. I wonder what she's waiting for.

"Oh… sorry… Louisa," I say, shaking her hand. Her nails are long, and almost certainly fake. Her eyes are made up beautifully, although the thick mascara is clumping just a little. Like me, she is dressed quite expensively, in what she might also hope is a casual manner. Is this what I look like? Only older, and less beautiful. This woman Stacey can get away with it. I'm starting to doubt that I can.

"Nice to meet you, Louise," she says. "New in town?"

"Sort of," I say, not bothering to correct her about my name. I cast my eyes back to the screen of my phone, hoping she will take the hint. She doesn't.

"Me too. Come down from near the border, me and my boys. Sean – that's my husband – got a job down here. It's a bit cheaper than some other bits of Cornwall, isn't it? Get more bang for your buck."

Oh, there are lots of words and phrases, and mispronunciations, that I hate, this being one of them. But I have to acknowledge that it is probably my problem more than anyone else's.

"Love this place, though!" she says, twirling a strand of blonde hair around her fingers. "A coffee shop downstairs… and the restaurants, too. I know there's not loads of choice, but it's not bad. The boys love the Mexican."

She's clearly got some cash to spend. I wonder what it

is that her husband does. But next to some of the people I've worked with and for over the years – with their London townhouses, yachts, and incredibly dull dinner parties with half the guests snorting white powder up their noses, men with women half their age attached to their arms – perhaps Stacey and Sean pale in comparison.

"We wanted to get them into private school," Stacey continues, as though I've asked, "but we're putting up with the local ones for now."

"That's where I went," I say, my back put firmly up.

"Oh? I thought you said you'd just moved here?"

"Moved back here," I clarify. "I've moved back from London."

"Oh, I love London," she gushes. "So much going on."

"Yes, although when you live and work there, you don't necessarily make the most of it." I turn my eyes back to my screen once more.

"Are you busy?" she asks.

"I'm... no, not really," I sigh, thinking I can't really claim to be. I am clearly only looking at Facebook. Although I have been using it to look for local walking groups. Could it really be that I am considering becoming a rambler? What would my former colleagues say if they knew?

"Great," she says. "I'm a lady of leisure, too."

Oh god.

"Maybe we can do this regularly..." she suggests.

Do what? My sarcastic inner voice wants to ask. But I know what she's saying. And I am not quite sure how I can find a reason to say no.

"Maybe." I look at the time on my phone and feign my

best surprised look. "I'd better get going. Sorry."

"Oh." Stacey looks a little bit put-out. Perhaps I'm not the first person to be keen to get away from her.

"Yes, sorry. It's my mum. She's quite old, and she lives nearby, and it's getting on for lunchtime..." It's not often that I flounder, but I find myself doing so now. As if Mum needs help getting her lunch ready! She'd have a few choice words to say if she heard me suggesting that she did.

"Oh, OK. Well, I'll give you a knock in a couple of days, yeah?"

"Erm, yes, fine." In the absence of any ready reason to say no, I seem to have no choice but to agree. "I'd better go, though. Bye, Stacey. Nice to meet you."

"Nice to meet you too, Louise."

1971

London was just as thrilling as Louisa had hoped it would be. Her feet ached with all the walking, and she found herself surprised that her mum needed a map to get around.

"I thought you were born here!"

"Well, yes, but not in the middle of London. And besides, I was only ten when I went to Cornwall with Whiteleys. Not old enough to get around London on my own – and far too long ago for me to remember where anything is!"

On the first night, after a journey of around six hours, they checked into their hotel and walked out in the early evening light to a small restaurant called Bocca Felice. The hotelier had recommended it – "It's Italian for 'happy mouth'," he had smiled. "Isn't that wonderful? And the food is, too."

Bocca Felice was a small, dark place, run by a friendly, short Italian man who had grey hair and a bald spot. He directed them to a table by the window. "Your first time here?" he asked.

"Yes," said Louisa politely.

"You like London?"

"Very much," said Louisa.

"I'm from London," Elise said. "Although I have not been for some time. It's changed a lot."

"It's a beautiful city. I come here after the war. I never go home."

Louisa and Elise pored over the menu. "I'll stick with fish," Elise said, seeing salmon listed, served with roast potatoes. Louisa ordered the lasagne, feeling quite shy and self-conscious in pronouncing it, but the waiter assured her she had said it perfectly.

There were breadsticks in a glass, but neither Elise nor Louisa knew if they were there for decoration, or to be eaten, or if they would have to pay extra for the privilege, so they left them untouched. Elise drank a small beer, which she would never do at home, while Louisa had a lemonade. Seated by the window, they had a view of a little square, and all the people going to and fro, at first dressed like office workers, and over time more like people heading out for an evening. Couples strolling arm in arm, or groups of glamorous-looking girls. There was all manner of people in London, and Louisa felt safe looking at them from her seat by the window. It seemed that Elise felt the same.

They talked a little, mostly about their food, and for dessert they each had a scoop of ice-cream (or *gelato*, as it was listed on the menu).

"Poor Laurie," Elise had said. "Missing out."

"It was his choice!" Louisa responded indignantly. "He could have come."

"He could. But I knew he wouldn't."

"It's nice being just you and me," Louisa said.

"Well that much is true," Elise had smiled.

After dinner they had gone for a little walk, through the greenery of the square and around the block, but as darkness started to pour in, Louisa began to feel a little nervous and out of place, and she was glad when Elise suggested they head back to the hotel for the night.

It was a twin-bedded room and there was a little kettle on a stand in the corner. Louisa had never stayed in a hotel before. She wasn't sure if Elise had, although she seemed to know what she was doing. They put the kettle on and made a cup of tea each, both turning up their noses at the unusual taste of the UHT milk.

There was a bathroom across the hall, and Louisa felt a bit strange using it, worrying that somebody else could knock on the door, but nobody did. She brushed her teeth then scurried back to the room and got under the covers while Elise took her turn in the bathroom. Again, Louisa felt a bit odd, in an unfamiliar room on her own, and particularly when she heard a man's voice in the corridor, but he and his companion passed right on by, and when Elise came back, she locked the door. They read for a while and then Elise turned out the light.

"Night, Lou," came Elise's voice.

"Night, Mum."

Louisa snuggled down, wishing she had taken the bed closer to the window. She could see an orange glowing outline around the bottom of the door, and she stared at it, watching for a shadow in case anyone stood outside, but the line of light remained unbroken, and in time she felt her eyes become heavy as she gave in to sleep.

The next day was a whirl of activity, beginning with a breakfast the likes of which Louisa had never seen before, with a choice of tea or coffee, which was brought to you at your table. As she chose tea and Elise selected coffee, both had their very own pot each. Then there was a full English, and then toast with butter and marmalade or jam.

"We won't be able to eat again all day," Elise said appreciatively, patting her full tummy, but by lunchtime

Louisa was more than ready for a sandwich and a bag of crisps, her appetite the product of a few hours' walking. That day they saw Buckingham Palace, St Paul's Cathedral, the Natural History Museum, the Victoria and Albert, and they had a walk along the side of the Thames, marvelling at the differences and similarities between this place and their little harbour back home. Louisa hadn't expected gulls in a city, but there were plenty, and their cries created a strange feeling in Louisa. A familiarity, and an almost homesickness. There were plenty of pigeons too. Not just at Trafalgar Square, although there was certainly an excess of them there, as they discovered later that afternoon.

In the evening, Louisa was surprised to discover that Elise had booked tickets for a show.

"Isn't this really expensive, Mum?" Louisa had asked.

The show was a musical called *Company*, and was funny and clever, and Louisa found herself utterly enthralled – so much so that she was shocked when it was time for the interval.

That her mum had selected a show with such a mature topic – it was about a 35-year-old single man and his friends, and their relationships – was a matter of pride for teenage Louisa. In fact, Elise's boss Mr Fawcett had booked the tickets, as a treat for his favourite employee, and he knew nothing about the show except that it had received excellent reviews. As it happened, the subject matter was hugely relevant to Elise, who had never entered a serious or long-term relationship again after Davey. It stayed with Louisa a long time, but when she went to see the show again three decades later, she

43

realised just how much had gone over her head.

By the time she crawled into bed that night, Louisa was already half-asleep, and far too tired to worry about the other hotel guests. Besides, after a day traversing the capital, she was feeling far more mature, cosmopolitan, and sophisticated.

In the morning, she and Elise had another breakfast and then had to make their way to Paddington, and back onto the Cornish Riviera Express, headed for home. As Elise settled in her seat, tired and ready to get forty winks, Louisa's mind wouldn't settle. She was buzzing with the thrill of the city, and all that she had seen and heard. A 'melting pot' of people, she had heard it called, and now she had seen it for herself, she knew that the term fitted it precisely.

She felt grubby and worn, and was looking forward to a long, hot bath back home that evening, but it felt like something had awoken within her and it was going to be very hard to push it back down or keep it quiet.

Louisa

It's a long week. I am almost tempted to knock on Stacey's door. Almost, but not quite.

Instead, I sit down to fill in the application form for the food hub. It's been quite some time since I have had to apply for a job, but this is not exactly taxing.

Name – easy.

Contact phone number/ email – easy.

Availability – any time. But maybe I shouldn't sound too available.

Can you drive/do you have a vehicle? Yes, I can drive; yes, I have a vehicle.

Please tell us a bit about why you'd like to volunteer/ which role interests you. This is the bit that takes some thought. There are four roles to choose from: Depot Assistant, Van Driver, Surplus Food Collector, and Pantry Front of House (making it sound like a restaurant – which actually I quite like). While I am mulling over what I'd like to do, my phone goes. It's Mum.

"Hi," I say, realising I sound a bit offhand. I am not, after all, in the office anymore. I know I was often short with Mum on the phone, and impatient, too. I need to be better at giving her my time. I certainly have plenty more of it these days. "How are you, Mum?"

"I'm a bit tired," she says. "But other than that, I'm absolutely fine."

"Too many late nights out on the town?"

"Well, not out on the town," she says, as if she goes out wandering the beaches at night.

"Hopefully you can have a siesta later." Ada has got Mum calling her afternoon rests siestas, as she was never entirely happy having 'naps' or 'Nanna naps', as my daughter cheekily calls them. If I'm honest, the idea of a little rest after lunch is becoming increasingly enticing to me as well, but perhaps just because it's a way of passing the time. I must not succumb. Mum is not the only one worried about letting age take over. I am in my mid-sixties, which I find hard to believe sometimes. Where did those years go? And I probably have at least a year's worth of sleep to catch up on, from the late nights at my desk, and the early starts – but I don't think it works like that.

Being here still feels a little bit like a holiday – and perhaps that's how I should be treating it, in fact, rather than already trying to fill as many hours as I can, with volunteering and wholesome activities. I just feel guilty if I'm not busy. I've emailed the man who runs the rambling club, and I've even popped down to the surf school. Ada would laugh her head off if I told her this. Or she may be proud. No, she'd definitely laugh her head off.

"Almost certainly," says Mum. "But first, I was phoning to invite you out on Saturday."

"That sounds nice."

"With Maggie and Stevie," she continues ever-so-slightly tentatively. "If you'd like to? It was Maggie's idea, actually." I feel like Mum is trying to placate me, as though knowing Maggie had invited me will make me like her more. It's not that I dislike the woman. I barely know her. I just don't necessarily actively like her, either. And there is the added complication of her being with Tony. That is a bit awkward, to say the least.

Still – this is another chance to make things easier for Mum. I put a smile on my face and hope that it lifts my voice. "That was nice of her. What's the plan?"

"Nothing fancy! Just a trip out of town, a walk on the beach, and a bag of chips. Fish and chips, if you like. My treat."

"OK," I say, not having any valid excuse to say no.

"Oh great!" Mum sounds genuinely delighted. "You'll love Maggie when you get to know her."

We'll see.

I hand in my application form in person. I want to see the food hub in action, and make sure I've selected the right options in terms of the roles I've applied for. I have said I'd be interested in Front of House and Surplus Food Collector. Although I am very happy living alone (I don't think I could share with anyone again, save for Ada), I do miss the contact with other human beings that I used to have at work. I had my own office – and I may have had the door shut, a lot – but I'd be on the phone with colleagues and clients, or pinging emails back and forth. I could wander down the hallway to the kitchen and be sure of a brief conversation or even a bit of subtle eavesdropping. I felt like there wasn't time to take a breath sometimes and yet I miss that, in a way.

The food-collecting also gives me a valid reason to get

out of town and reacquaint myself with Cornwall, whilst doing something good. It must be my daughter's influence (she gets into everything), but I am feeling increasingly guilty about having a car, and I consider all my journeys carefully. I came down here determined to walk or use public transport as much as possible, but silly me, I'd forgotten how limiting that can be. I'm used to buses and trains every couple of minutes. A tap of the Oyster card, and I'd be on my way. Even if a tube's full, it's normally just a matter of minutes before the next one comes along. I think wistfully of that feeling, that rush of air when you're on the platform and a train's just gone through. People say London is a lonely place to be, but I don't think that is necessarily true. I always felt a part of something; a huge organism, constantly evolving as people moved in and out of the city. Yes, it's not really the done thing to make eye contact on the tube, and it's unusual to greet random people with a cheery hello, when you pass them on the street, but perhaps that's because there are so many people. It would take forever. We all had different things going on, and for lots of people it's a live-and-let-live kind of thing. I knew my neighbours well enough to say hello to, or take in a parcel for them if they were out, and very occasionally I had been round to one of their houses for a Christmas Eve drink, but that was that. Fine by me.

I am hopeful that getting out and about around Cornwall and meeting different people will give me back a bit of that. And these will be transactional relationships – very little effort required on either side. Very little depth, but that's not a problem to me.

"Hi Louisa!" I am greeted by Jude, and I'm impressed she's remembered my name. Her blue eyes are on me, and I feel like I'm being assessed. "You came back, then!"

This is incorrect, as this is the first time I've been to the depot, or 'HQ' as Tamsin calls it. I let it slide. "Yes. And I've brought my form in."

"Fantastic! So what is it you'd like to do?"

I explain I've selected two roles.

"That is extra fantastic, thank you so much. We'll just need to arrange a time for an interview, and then hopefully get you on some training asap."

Training? It's bad enough they want to interview me. Although I can grudgingly acknowledge that it does show an admirable level of professionalism.

"Great," I say, handing over my form in its pristine plastic wallet.

"Beautiful presentation," she smiles. "Looks like you're no stranger to office work."

If only you knew, I think. I suppose they'll ask in the interview.

"Thanks." I look more closely at Jude. She's perhaps a little bit younger than I am, but not all that much. Her skin is clear and smooth, with just a few laughter lines at the corners of her eyes. She appears to be make-up-free. Today, she is dressed in jeans and a sweatshirt. I feel overdressed in my denim shirt-dress, tights and boots, even though these are the kinds of thing I wear when I'm dressing down. At home, I'll happily wear pyjamas and loungewear, but I wouldn't be seen dead outside the house in a pair of sweatpants. Well, not unless I was going to the gym – something I have not done in years. Maybe I ought to restart that now I've got

49

all this time to fill. I could be the fittest I've ever been.

"Right, well leave this with me, and I'll be in touch," she says.

"Oh, I was... I was quite hoping to be able to have a look around."

"I'm sorry," she says, "we're rushed off our feet today, and down a couple of volunteers. When you come for interview, I'll show you around properly. OK?"

"That's fine, thank you." I'm not used to being given the brush-off like this. I walk out of the hub and get in the car. It's a windy day, autumn pressing its advantage now. As I drive back towards town, the sea is up in arms, waves chopping this way and that. Apparently it's not just me who is feeling restless.

I drive into the Saltings' private car park, into my allotted space.

"Louisa!" I hear somebody call from behind me. I already recognise the voice. Tony. I suppose this was bound to happen sooner or later.

"Oh, hi."

"How are you?" he asks. "Settling in?"

"Yes, I think so."

"I suppose this is just coming home to you though, anyway?"

"Well, yes. Although... it's been a long time. It's a different world to what I'm used to."

"I know what you mean. I'm loving it, though."

I can see it does suit him. He's got a tan, and he looks relaxed. His shirt is open at the collar, and he's wearing some fairly casual navy trousers. It's a far cry from the buttoned-up, suited and booted Tony I knew in London.

"Listen, do you want to grab a coffee? In the café, or up

in my office? I know it's a bit weird, us both being here. I'd prefer it if it wasn't, though."

I pause. "OK. Thanks. Maybe your office?"

"Scared people will talk?" he grins.

"You have no idea! You don't know this place like I do."

"True. I feel like I'm getting a pretty good idea of it, though."

"Will Maggie mind?"

"No! At least, I don't think so. She's pretty cool about things."

Practically perfect, I think, but tell myself not to be so childish. She's probably just a really nice person. She must be, if Mum and Tony think so highly of her.

We get the lift up to Tony's floor. "I normally try to take the stairs," he says. "Need to keep this trim physique." He's not in bad shape, actually. Then again, he's younger than me. (Isn't everyone? It certainly seems that way.)

"That's not a bad idea. I should do the same when I'm going to my flat. I've been thinking about joining the gym," I admit.

"No! Is this what happens when you stop work?"

"Apparently."

He lets me into the office, holding the door open for me. Ada considers that kind of gesture redundant. A sexist throwback. Depending on the person doing it, I generally don't mind at all. It's polite. I will hold the door open for other people, men or women.

I find I can't help smiling as I walk in and am greeted by the floor-to-ceiling windows framing the view of the unruly sea.

"Wow!" I exclaim.

"It's not that different from your flat's," he says, and of

course, he's been in my flat, when it was an empty shell. Probably numerous times.

"True. But it's bigger. And it's incredible for an office."

"I know. I'm a bit gutted I'll have to hand it over in a year or so's time. Just have to make the most of it while I'm here."

"Will you stay? In Cornwall?"

"I don't know. Maybe. I'd like to. It has to depend on work a bit, though," he says ruefully.

"There's more and more working remotely now," I remind him. "I'm sure you can get something to suit you."

"Yeah, I wouldn't mind being in the city a day or two a week. I do miss it sometimes. I'd like the best of both worlds."

"I understand, believe me. And you're about to face your first Cornish winter... buckle in!"

"Is it that bad?"

"No, it's not. I like to be here in the winter. It's very peaceful, and it can be warm when the rest of the country's freezing. You get some fantastic storms as well."

"We had one of them in the summer," he says. "Isn't it amazing being by the sea when the weather's taking control?"

"It is." I smile at how easy he is making this. "It's good to see you, Tony."

"You too."

"And you seem happy."

"I am. Thank you. Latte?"

"Please."

He's got his own fancy coffee machine, rather than an assistant to make his coffee. As he taps away at the touchscreen, he says, "I haven't said anything to Maggie, about anything."

"Oh. OK."

"I know it's a bit weird, what with her being friends with your mum. I just wanted to let you know I won't be saying anything, to Maggie, about what happened."

"Oh right, thanks. But that is really up to you." I feel uncomfortable with the line this conversation is taking. Like I have something to be ashamed of. "It's just a bit odd, I suppose. I'd actually told Mum I was in a relationship with somebody. And I suppose I feel a bit embarrassed about everything."

"You shouldn't." He hands me my coffee.

"Thanks. And I do know that, really. Suddenly, I feel quite old, though. And stupid. I got ahead of myself, like some kind of over-excited teenager."

"Not that old then!"

We both laugh.

"Anyway," Tony smiles at me. I am so glad there is not a trace of sympathy there – just kindness. "I just wanted to reassure you. You can trust me. And you can talk to me, any time, if you want to."

I won't be doing that, but it's nice of him to say so. I smile and ask him about work, signalling that this topic of conversation is over.

It's good to hear what Tony has to say, and catch up on news from the office. Now I've left the place, I feel more attached to it, and more interested in my ex-colleagues' lives than I ever was when I was actually working with them. When I notice Tony looking at his watch, I kick myself. "Sorry, I'm sure you need to get on."

"It's only that I've got a call in a few minutes. You know

what it's like," he says apologetically. I put my cup on the gleaming glass table, and I stand up. Tony walks to the door with me and it seems like he's about to hug me. I don't want that. I hurriedly thank him for the coffee and the chat, then leave, taking the stairs down to the ground floor.

I know Maggie's office is on the first floor, and I'm intrigued to know more about where she works, but that really is none of my business. The wind tries to snatch the door from me as I walk outside. The moored boats are rocking determinedly, like they're trying to free themselves.

A kind-looking, moustachioed man grabs hold of the door, helping me tame it. "They need to sort this out!" he says, smiling at me. "Now they're making some money from it, they seem less eager to please."

"That sounds about right." I don't mention I was one of 'them' until not very long ago.

It takes less than a minute to get back to my place. I can see Stacey heading towards me on the harbourside, so I pretend not to have seen her, then I scurry in and towards the stairs, just so I don't have to share the lift with my new neighbour. A good idea of Tony's, this. The stairs can serve a dual purpose, helping me to keep fit and avoid the neighbours at the same time. Two birds with one stone.

1971

Laurie was in a funny mood when they returned. Louisa wondered if he was jealous about her trip with their mum, but he had also had the chance to come along, and he had opted not to, so that was his lookout.

He had stayed on his own at Godolphin Terrace but, unlike many of their peers, there was no chance he would have used the opportunity to have friends over – or a girl. Louisa almost laughed at the thought of that, although it did make her feel a little bit sad as well. He was a good brother, and they got on well most of the time. She knew life wasn't as easy for him as it should be. And now Maudie was coming round talking to Elise about Laurie in hushed tones. Louisa had tried to listen, but all she had heard was a handful of words... among them her brother's name, and *upset*, and *empty bottle*.

What had gone on while they were away? She needed to know.

"Mum..." she tried Elise first.

"Yes, Lou?"

"Is Laurie OK?"

Elise looked slightly pained at this question. She took a moment, as though considering her answer. "He's alright, love, don't worry. Just... some difficult stuff. Well, it's hard growing up, isn't it?"

This was an unsatisfactory answer.

She tried Maudie, who she knew had a soft spot for her.

"Maudie..."

"Yes, my love?"

"Was Laurie alright when we were away? I feel like he's upset about something." Nice work on the concerned sister front. Although it wasn't entirely a front. But if she was very honest, her driving force was nosiness as much as anything.

Maudie, frustratingly, was as tight-lipped as her mum. There was only one thing for it. She would have to ask Laurie himself.

"Can I come with you?" she asked him, on Sunday afternoon, when he was packing all his birdwatching paraphernalia.

This alone was enough to rouse Laurie's suspicions, but he was also feeling a bit down, and a bit lonely, and the thought of some company – even if it was only his little sister – was cheering.

"Are you sure you want to come? I'm planning to be out a few hours."

"Yes. It's a beautiful day. And I feel a bit grimy after London. Some fresh air and sunshine will make it all better."

"Sure," he said, his mind galloping away to a world where his sister began to share his passion for all things wildlife.

Louisa packed a bag with some crisps, apples, wedges of cake, and a book. She put her swimming costume on, just in case they ended up somewhere she could have a dip – or at the very least do a bit of sunbathing.

Elise watched from the window in wonder, as her two children strode purposefully away together.

They walked in silence at first, trudging up and out of town along the rugged path that would take them around the edge of the estuary. The tide was out, and the sandbanks glistened in the sunshine.

"What do you want to look for?" Laurie asked eagerly. "Waders?"

"You tell me," said Louisa. "I'm happy to do whatever you want to do."

Laurie smiled. He did love his little sister. He just knew that she was different to him. Could better him at most things. And although she was younger, she was already so much more worldly-wise. But this was one area where he had the upper hand. Sea life, wildlife, the natural world.

"OK, well, I know a great little spot, sheltered–" he knew she would want to get in some sunbathing if she could – "and we could set up there. I'm keeping a record of unusual sightings. I saw a ruff the other week!" he added excitedly.

"Really?" Louisa asked, having no idea about many birds at all.

"Yes, maybe we'll see him again today. Males have these great big plumes of feathers round their necks, that's why they're called ruffs, I suppose, and they're pretty rare around these parts. They're normally in the east of the country. Here–" he got out his favourite bird book, and turned to a page with a bent corner – "this is what they look like. See if you can spot one before me. Your eyesight's better than mine!"

Louisa had rarely seen her brother so animated. She felt a sudden pull of love for him, so strong it brought tears to her eyes, surprising her.

"I'll do my best," she smiled. But she had not forgotten her motivation for coming with him. She just had to find the right moment.

Fiddling with his second-best pair of binoculars, she said, "This is what makes you happy, isn't it?"

"Yes," Laurie said seriously, looking at her. "It is. It does."

"And are you unhappy, generally?" She let her words out without allowing herself time to rethink.

"Unhappy?" He looked genuinely intrigued by the question. "No. I don't think so. I—" he looked at her, seeing where she was going. "You want to know what happened, don't you? When you were away?"

Louisa felt her face flush. Was she that obvious?

"Is that why you've come with me this afternoon?"

"No, I—"

"I don't mind. It's still nice to have you here."

There was that rush of love again.

"I'm just worried about you, Laurie. I know we don't talk much. And yes, I do want to know. I want to know you're OK." It was true, as much as she wanted to know what had happened to satisfy her own curiosity, she really did want to know that her brother was alright.

"I'm fine. Honestly. I just did something... stupid."

"What?"

"Well, I got drunk, I suppose."

"Drunk? You?" She couldn't hide her incredulous reaction.

"Yes!" he laughed. "I know. Completely out of character. Maudie came to drop off some tea and she found me passed out in the lounge. In full view of the window. Embarrassing, really," he muttered.

"Oh no, Laurie. Did you have anyone else with you?" Louisa wondered if she'd been wrong in thinking he wouldn't take advantage of having the house to himself.

Maybe he did have a secret girlfriend. Maybe even a boyfriend?

"No! Who would I have invited? I'm not exactly Mr Popular!"

The pain. It was almost tangible. Louisa was beginning to wish that she had left well enough alone. She wasn't qualified to deal with this. But then, he was her brother. And if not her, then who?

"Why did you get so drunk?" she asked, tentatively.

"I wanted to know why he did it."

"Who?"

"Dad," he said bitterly. "Our dad. I wanted to know how he felt."

"Dad used to get drunk?" Louisa asked, shocked.

"Just a bit," Laurie replied drily. "Only on weekends. And weekdays." He'd heard somebody else say that line and he'd been waiting for a chance to use it.

"Oh." Louisa didn't know what to say.

"Dad was a bastard."

"What?"

"A bastard," he confirmed flatly. "I hated him."

Louisa was shocked. Her memories of her dad were vague and not fully formed, but she hadn't known this about him. And their mother had never suggested there was anything untoward about him. She would surely have told Louisa if there was. Perhaps Laurie was wrong.

"But you were so young. How can you remember?"

"I can't forget how he made me feel. I was scared of him, Lou. I think Mum was, too. You're too young to remember him properly. And she won't speak ill of him now, though I wish she bloody would. Honestly, I'm never getting married. I'm never having kids."

"But why not?"

"What if I'm the same as him? I couldn't stand it."

Something clicked in Louisa's mind. She had wondered why her big brother was like he was. She wanted to hug him, but his posture was rigid, and he was flicking through his bird book, back and forth, back and forth. She didn't know if he would welcome physical contact.

"You'd never be like that, Laurie," she'd said instead, still reeling from the revelation, but sure that whatever the truth of the matter, her brother was a strong, kind and gentle boy.

"Who knows? But we'll never find out," he said firmly. "You'll be the one to have the family, and I can be your kids' uncle, OK?"

"OK," she'd agreed.

And they had left it at that. Louisa kept thinking of questions but felt unsure of herself, and of him. Laurie had got drunk. That was unimaginable. She and her friends talked about sneaking a few drinks sometime, but had never actually done it yet.

She wanted to ask Laurie what it felt like, but sensed that it was perhaps not the most sensitive question. Instead, she moved next to him. "Show me that picture again," she said, "of the ruff. Let's see if we can spot him."

"OK," he agreed, and that was that.

They sat in their secluded spot together, Louisa asking questions about the birds they saw, and even the plants that surrounded them, swaying in the gentle breeze and tickling their skin. She fell asleep for a while, and Laurie didn't wake her but looked at his sister, grateful for her, and grateful that she didn't remember their dad.

On the way back home, while the spring sun was only just beginning to arc back down towards the horizon, Louisa risked one more question: "Why did Mum stay with him?"

"She had to, didn't she? It's what people did. But she stood up to him, sometimes. Protected you, and me."

That made some kind of sense. The Mum Louisa knew would not have just let somebody hurt her. Much less her children. But still, she could have left him. She could, surely. She had friends. Maudie. And Angela. Louisa knew a little about life, she thought. She knew there were men who beat their wives, and their children. She knew it was wrong. But to think this was what had happened in her own family was prompting all sorts of uncomfortable questions, which were just beginning to prick at her consciousness. Why would Elise have stayed with a husband who hurt her, and who scared her children – her son, at least? It seemed weak, somehow, and Louisa did not want to think of her mum that way.

She let these thoughts drift through her mind, but she didn't quite dare to voice them to Laurie. He had been through enough. And it was nice, sitting with him, calmly and peacefully. She didn't think she could get into birdwatching in the way that he was, but she could see the appeal of the odd quiet afternoon like this one.

"Can we do this again, Laurie?"

"Of course!" he exclaimed delightedly. "Any time. Every weekend, if you like!"

"I don't think I'd go that far," she smiled, and he laughed, his fringe falling across his eyes. She wanted to sweep it away and reveal just who her brother could be, if only he were more sure of himself.

When they arrived home, Elise was waiting for them smilingly, delighted that they had spent the afternoon together. She hugged them both. "Did you have a good time?"

"Yes thanks," said Louisa, but she found she could barely look at her mum. The revelations from Laurie had dredged up some uncomfortable feelings. "I need to get changed before tea," she said, heading straight upstairs. She needed time to think, to clear her mind, and work out exactly how she felt.

Louisa

If I'd thought about it, I'd have found a reason to have driven myself. Now here I am in the back of Maggie's old car, sitting with an eleven-year-old who keeps thrusting her phone in front of me to show me TikToks. Each time she does it, I have to refocus my eyes, and smile and nod or laugh as appropriate. She's a nice girl, Stevie – delightful, in fact – but I'm not really a TikTok kind of person. And there's Mum sitting up front with Maggie, chatting away and having a lovely time.

Still, it's kind of them to invite me, and I surprised myself by finding I was actually looking forward to today. It's good to have somebody else planning things so that I can just tag along.

Maggie picked me and Mum up from Godolphin Terrace. I felt a bit embarrassed at the thought of them collecting me from the Saltings. On the way to Mum's, I picked up some sweets for Stevie, and a bunch of flowers for Maggie. I could see Mum was pleased about this.

"How are you, Louisa? Settling in OK?" Maggie's eyes are on mine via the car's rear-view mirror.

"Yes thanks. It's quite funny being so high up, though. I mean, I'm really lucky, and it's an incredible view, but it feels a bit lofty – and a bit remote, in a way."

"Well, if you're ever feeling too remote and I'm in the office, give me a shout. We could go and have a coffee or something."

"Thanks, Maggie. I might just do that." I won't.

I gaze out of the window as we make our way through the little lanes and down towards the coast once more. When we draw up at the beach car park, Stevie puts her phone away.

"I wish we had a dog," she says to me.

"Do you?" I've never seen the attraction myself.

"Yeah... I want someone to run on the beach with. Mum's never up for running, are you, Mum?"

"What's that? Running? No, not anymore. It's too hard to run on the sand anyway. It's alright when you're small and light, like you."

"So why don't we get a dog? They're small and light. Or they can be."

I admire Stevie's line of argument, and her directness.

"Who's going to look after it while I'm at work and you're at school? It would get lonely."

"It can come and be in the office with you. Lots of places let you take dogs into work."

"How do you know that? Don't tell me... TikTok!" Maggie laughs and her eyes meet mine in the mirror once more.

"No... not just TikTok..." Stevie is outraged. "Would you walk it for us, Louisa? If we had one. You haven't got a job."

"Stevie!"

"What? I'm just asking."

"Putting Louisa on the spot, more like! I'm sure she has plenty of better ways to fill her time than walking our imaginary dog." I don't. "Sorry, Louisa."

"Not at all," I say. "If you don't ask, you don't get. But don't take that to mean I would walk your dog for you, Stevie. Your mum's right. If you get an animal, you need to know you can take care of all its needs."

Where's that come from? What do I know about keeping animals? I allowed Ada to have a hamster once, but it died after a short four months. It was a painful and disappointing experience for us both – and probably for the hamster, too.

"I'd walk him for you if I could," Mum says.

"Mum! You're not helping matters," I say, and Maggie and I glance at each other. I feel a momentary comradeship. Her versus her daughter. Me versus my mother. "Honestly, your generation have no sense of responsibility." This makes everyone laugh. I feel strangely elated.

We bundle out of the car and into our coats. It's a slightly dull day. Not much wind, but not much blue sky, either. Nevertheless, it's good to be on the beach. We could have gone to one of our beaches at home of course, but I do appreciate getting out of town. I think perhaps we all feel the same.

Stevie runs down the path onto the expanse of sand, and I can see how a dog would make a good companion for her. Maggie is still light on her feet, though; Mum less so. I'm somewhere in between. I don't think any of us are a good match for Stevie.

"How's Stevie getting on at secondary school?" I ask.

"She's alright now she's found her way around," Maggie smiles, pushing her hair out of her eyes, "and realised that timetables too terrifying."

"And has she made new friends?"

"Some, I think. But she's sticking with the ones she knows from primary as well."

"No harm in that. Ada's still best friends with Clara, and they've been that way since they were eight."

"That's lovely. As is Ada, by the way. She's been so good to Stevie."

"I think she genuinely enjoys her company. But it's nice to hear, thank you."

Mum is walking a few steps behind us, and I turn to see that she's OK. She smiles at me. I can see that she's relaxed, just taking it all in – the sights, sounds and smells. The breeze on her skin, in her hair. It must be strange being her age. She might very well have a good few years left in her. I certainly hope so. But I know I am increasingly aware of my own mortality, so when you're as advanced in years as my mum, you must know you might not have many left. I feel like she takes more of an interest in everything, like she's trying to imprint it all on her mind. I suppose she's scared of losing her mobility or her marbles, or both. I am grateful that at the moment she is fit and healthy, and able to get around.

We walk the full length of the beach, Stevie collecting interesting shells and stones and handing them to her mum. I notice Maggie subtly dropping some of them back onto the sand, and she smiles at me conspiratorially. "I do keep a few," she says, "but we'd have a beach of our own at home if I kept everything she picks up on our walks."

I laugh. "So how's Tony?" I don't mention that I saw him the other day but I am asking out of genuine interest. Maggie seems like a good match for him.

"Oh, he's fine, thanks!" she smiles. "Isn't it weird, that you two already know each other?"

"Yes, and now we're both here, on the other side of the country!" I agree. "It is a bit odd. This place has quite a draw though, doesn't it? Cornwall, I mean."

"Totally. I'm from Bristol originally. My sister and I were born there but our parents wanted to move closer to the sea. When Dad got the chance to work in Cornwall, they jumped at it."

"And is your mum still moving down here?"

"Yes, she's completing soon, actually."

"Well, that's exciting."

"It is... and stressful... you know what it's like, moving."

"Only too well."

"But it'll be nice to have her close by."

"Am I right in thinking that my neighbours are from up your way, too?"

I think I detect a slight drop in Maggie's expression. "Oh, you mean Stacey and Sean? I did wonder if you might have met yet. Yes... well, only Stacey, really. I've known her a long time. She moved away for a while, and came back with Sean."

"She's quite forthright, isn't she?"

"That's one way of putting it. She's more Julia's – my sister's – friend than mine, though."

"Oh?"

"Yeah, they just have more in common, I guess."

I don't know Maggie's sister, but I can already see that Maggie and Stacey are cut from a different cloth.

"It's a small world," I observe.

"It certainly seems to be. Typical they've got one of the

new places in the Saltings, though... sorry, I didn't mean..."

"No problem. I know what you meant."

I know I sound like I'm bristling, and I'm really not. I do know what she means. And I've wondered myself, more than once, about my choice of home. I think I wanted to keep that distinction drawn, of being a bit different from most of the town. I may be born and bred here, but I am not the person I was when I left. God, a lot of people have barely ever left Cornwall for as much as a weekend. I've worked and lived in London for decades, plus a year or so in Singapore. The apartment is a status symbol for me, as I suppose Stacey and Sean's is for them. I really can see Maggie's point of view. Nevertheless, it's up to us where we choose to live.

We fall silent for a while. Then Maggie says, "Did you know Tony very well? When you worked together?"

I can't tell if this is an innocent question, if she suspects something has happened involving Tony and me, or if she's just trying to glean some information about her relatively new partner.

"Fairly well. I mean, we did work together quite a lot, and put in a lot of long hours. I appreciated having him around. The Americans could be hard work."

"Yes, he did say he's not a fan of the guys you were working with."

"He's a good judge of character! He's a good man."

That makes her smile. "I know."

"Does Stevie like him?"

"Yes, and so does Mum."

"Mums are always a good judge of character, too. At least, mine is." I find myself smiling at Maggie now. I do like her, and I hope she sees the compliment in my words. She's earnest, and a little unsure of herself. But she seems to be a good person. I've never been much of one for friends but I do wonder if she and I could be, one day. Maybe I'm getting ahead of myself.

"Your mum is a gem. And she's so happy you're back in Cornwall."

"I'm beginning to think I am, too."

The wind picks up as we retrace our steps along the beach, creating miniature sandstorms as it sweeps across the ground. The tide is creeping back towards the land and the light possesses a duskier quality. I'm glad of the warmth and stillness in the café, where we find a cosy table for four, and order chips, and cups of tea.

"Let me see my finds, Mum," Stevie says.

Maggie empties her pockets.

"Hey, where's that stone with the Cornish flag on it?"

"The...?"

"It had a little cross on it, like the flag." Stevie screws her face up with consternation and her eyebrows knit together. She looks cute. I wouldn't tell her that. No eleven-year-old wants to be cute.

"Oh, I'm sorry, love, I must have dropped it," Maggie says, and I hide my smile.

"Never mind, Stevie. Just pop back down to the beach and get it," I say.

"I'll never find it..." I see her expression change, like a cloud moving along to reveal the sun. "You're teasing, aren't you?"

"Maybe a little."

Stevie laughs good-naturedly. It's nice being around

somebody so young. It is only a handful of years since Ada was this age, but in that time she has blossomed and grown up and flown the nest, and all the other clichés. I find my stomach contracting at the thought of her, and how much I miss her. I can't wait for her to come and visit.

On the car journey home, my eyes feel heavy, and my cheeks feel like they've caught the sun, although there was precious little of it today. Stevie is busy on her phone, and I settle myself against the seat and the headrest, and allow myself to doze, glad now that I'm not driving. I must only have had ten minutes or so, but when I wake up we're on the outskirts of town. There is a very light mist just tiptoeing along the open spaces, looking to fill the gaps, and the streetlights are on. It's a sign that summer really is gone, but I don't mind. I'm an autumn kind of person. *In the autumn of my life*, I think ruefully. I hate all that stuff. Mum and Maggie are chatting away, and I keep quiet for a while, enjoying this feeling that I really have come home.

1980s

After Louisa had left home for university in Bristol (perhaps she had unknowingly crossed paths with Lucy back then), there had been no turning back. No coming back home, for her. Well, except for university breaks, but even then she began to return to her rented accommodation sooner, citing her part-time bar job as the reason, and the opportunity to be closer to the library.

Elise was disappointed, but not surprised. For a few years now, she had felt Louisa slowly peeling herself away from her and their life together. The girl had tried numerous images and lifestyle choices, from punk to hippy. She was testing things out, pushing boundaries and seeing how different she could make herself, from her mother and her brother.

Elise was no fool, and knew when her daughter returned home smelling of cigarette smoke or booze or cannabis, or all three. She kept her counsel and kept her cool. Better to see where it led, she thought, and step in if and when necessary.

Teenage Louisa had found older boyfriends for herself, and some locals discussed how she was maybe trying to find a father figure, but her boyfriends weren't that old, and Elise knew that it was more likely her daughter was just trying to annoy her mum.

But Louisa was not stupid. She was young, yes, and trying out having a wild side but ultimately, she was sensible. And try as she might, she could not prevent herself from being a driven, results-focused individual. She did very well in her exams, but said that she wanted to work rather than study further. A year into an admin role at a local solicitors, which was far too similar to her mum's life for her liking, she decided that actually she did want to further her studies. She applied successfully to Bristol University, for a degree in computer sciences. She was one of only two young women on her course, and she settled in very well. Having already tried out drink/drugs/sex to know exactly how she felt about them all, she politely withdrew from her peers, some of whom were only just discovering these things, and she worked as hard as she possibly could. By the time she came back to Cornwall at Christmas, she was as straight and studious as could be, and she spent much of the holidays reading. Laurie had already flown the nest by then, and spent his Christmas on Skomer, a small island off the coast of south Wales.

Even before she graduated, Louisa had been snapped up by a company in London, keen to increase the number of female employees and ready to take her on as soon as she had left student life behind. She had the confidence and will to drive a bargain even then, and she got them to agree to fund her Master's degree, and allow her a day's study leave each week.

Amongst her mainly male colleagues, she quickly became known as the Ice Queen – not the world's most original nickname. A couple of them had dared to ask her out, but had been quickly shunned. Lesbian was one verdict. Frigid another. She was neither of those things, although she did appreciate the beauty of women, and sometimes wished that she was attracted to them in that way. Having said that, she didn't find friendships easy, and she considered most of the other women at work frustrating; a bit weak. She had sat in meetings where she had been absolutely flabbergasted to hear a senior male colleague make comments about the size of his PA's breasts – *while she was sitting in the room, at the same table, as them.* The woman had turned red, but had good-naturedly laughed it off. Louisa had stood up and walked out. She'd heard the laughter as the door shut behind her.

What was wrong with people? She did realise that the young woman, who was in fact a couple of years older than her, was in a difficult situation. He was her boss, after all. It was him in the wrong, Louisa was in no doubt about that, but how could she just sit there and not put him straight? Laugh, as though it was acceptable and funny. *Boys will be boys.* How Louisa hated that sentiment. The longer they were allowed to get away with it, the more ingrained it became. She dreamed of starting her own, all-female, company. That would satisfy those idiots who thought she was a lesbian!

Still, she stuck it out. She worked long and hard, and put her head above the parapet regularly, to apply for promotions, and volunteer for projects. Clients loved her. Colleagues grudgingly respected her. Boyfriends found her strength a turn-on, although they never lasted too long. She wouldn't let them. Life was not going to be about relationships for Louisa. She was not going to land herself with some less-than-worthy man and a couple of kids, like her mother had.

She took a clinical, analytical approach to it all, examining the reasons why people had relationships in the first place.

1. **Love.** She wrote this off immediately.
2. **Attraction.** She could see this had its place, but it wouldn't last. It couldn't. Not once you started to find out the truth about that person you had been lusting after. The dirty clothes left on the floor. The unappealing eating habits. Irritating laugh. Unrealistic political beliefs. Unhealthy lifestyle. Drinking too much – well, she knew all about the damage that could do, thanks to her parents.
3. **Security.** She would provide that for herself, thank you very much.
4. **Starting a family.** This was so far from her radar, it was laughable.
5. **Companionship.** Unnecessary. She was quite happy in her own company, and anyone who wasn't the same was clearly lacking something.

Every now and then, she would like a boyfriend a little bit more than the others. Or she might find herself seeing somebody just as driven and determined as her, who seemed to respect her and also sometimes challenge her, and she might consider something longer, and stronger. But a little voice inside always told her it would be a mistake. Eventually, she knew, it would all come to nothing, and it would just be a big mess that needed to be tidied up. Better to keep relationships short, sweet and neat, parting on good terms whenever possible, and moving on.

She would not date married men, or men with girlfriends. Any man willing to do that would not be worthy of her time and attention anyway. Not that she was dead-set on monogamy, but she valued loyalty and trust highly.

She had a small group of friends, some from uni and some from her early days at work, but the uni friends were scattered geographically, and by and by it seemed that every single one of them found a partner, and settled down – usually they got married and within a year or so of the wedding were expecting their first child. This was all very well and good, and Louisa would send a card and flowers for the parents, and a book for the baby, but it was not for her.

Except... if she was very honest, motherhood wasn't absolutely always a million miles away from her thoughts. She might be on the tube, heading into the City for a tough day at work, or heading home from a long day in the office, and see a woman with a baby snuggling into her, or a toddler sleeping with chubby arms wrapped round their mother's neck, and she would feel a small but definite twang somewhere deep inside. She allowed herself to briefly imagine what it might be like to be needed and loved in that way. But she knew beyond a doubt that stopping work to have a baby was a sure-fire route to failure. Her peers would move on and up without her, and she would never again be considered for the serious projects. They (the men) would assume that her priority would be her child. And, she supposed, it should be.

There would be a gap in her pension payments, and her national insurance. She would lose out in so many ways, she rarely considered in what ways she might gain.

Louisa bought her own flat, in a time when the term 'yuppie' was in popular use. Was she young? Yes. Was she upwardly mobile? Yes, yes, yes. So what if people laughed at her, and Harry Enfield had some stupid character poking fun at the young and successful? She had made her own money, and she had no doubt that she deserved it. If some opinionated morons were jealous of her success, that was their problem.

She visited Cornwall twice a year – at Christmas, and for a week in the summer. Phone calls with Elise were regular but short. As their lives became increasingly different, Louisa didn't know what to talk about with her mother, who insisted on saying that Louisa 'worked in computers', which was not in the least bit correct.

But Elise too had done well at work, in her own small way, as she thought of it. She was an efficient, professional office manager for a small law firm, and she was well respected, and sometimes approached by other firms, which she always turned down. She too valued trust and loyalty. After Davey, there had been a few low-key dalliances, but she had not found another relationship – because she didn't want to. How Louisa could not see the similarities between the two of them was a mystery, but then Elise didn't see them, either. Her daughter almost scared her at times, she was so driven and single-minded.

But Elise had the benefit of age, and of having known Louisa as a small child. She knew the very roots of her girl, and held on to them tight. Some day, she hoped, Louisa would want to know them again herself.

Louisa

"So what do you think you will get out of volunteering?" Jude asks.

"Oh, I hadn't really thought of it as me getting something... more giving," I say, finding it hard to believe how disingenuous I sound, but unable to stop the words coming out of my mouth.

She just looks at me, a small smile on her face, which I could come to find infuriating. These kinds of places seem to attract a similar type of person. For a short while, pre-Ada, I had entertained the prospect of volunteering at a mental health helpline. I had gone along to the training sessions, but I had to concede it was not for me. It wasn't the people who were calling the helpline that put me off. It was the other volunteers. And the paid staff. In fact, they were the worst. I suppose I'm too impatient. I didn't have time in my life for all the *Mmm*ing, and *Uhuh*s. But by the same token, there were also some incredible people there. A woman whose son had taken his own life, which is just beyond words. She was a perfectly normal woman (by my standards) – hard-working, pleasant, well-dressed – and she was able to take what had happened to her and use it to try to prevent something similar happening to others. I've never forgotten her, actually. But the paid staff were either flaky, or had their heads so far up their own backsides they could see daylight. And I realised that not only did I not have the patience for it, but I would have struggled to honour the commitment they required, of four hours a week. It may not sound much, but my job was unpredictable, with long hours and occasional travel. If I'm really honest, I realised that I liked the idea of volunteering more than the reality.

I err against mentioning any of this now, and I merely smile back at Jude, who doesn't seem to notice my gritted teeth. She's got knowing eyes, though – as well as that smile. Still, I want this, I remind myself. I need it. I need something to do. And there's my answer.

"Well, as you know, I've just retired, from a very high-profile job, actually." I sound unbearable. I know I do. Jude merely maintains the smile. "And I've moved back here, and... well, I'm going to be honest. I'm a bit lost. I'm used to working all the hours, and now I'm trying to find things to fill them. And it's strange."

"I understand," Jude says. "I really do. And we find a lot of retired people like to help, whether it's just sorting stuff here at the depot, or getting out and about collecting. Now, I know you've put down two roles here, but I was thinking it might be good to start you on just the one. The surplus food collections."

"Oh?" I'm astounded. I'd have thought they'd be crying out for my help. Didn't she listen to me, about the career I've just left?

"Yes, and it's not that I don't think you can do the job."

I should bloody well hope not.

"But...?" I say.

"But I think it might be good for you to get the lie of the land a bit. It's quite a different world to the one you've come from."

"Yes, I'm well aware of that, thank you. I was, after all, born and raised here."

"I know all that." The smile again. "But it's been a while, hasn't it? I'm thinking that if we begin with the collections, and you decide you'd like to stay with us, you could shadow Tamsin a few times, to see what it's all about. Now, how about we look at the collections for next week, and work out which ones you can do? If you'd still like to volunteer with us, that is."

"I… yes." She's played me the way I play other people. She hasn't given me a chance to argue the toss, and she's given me a positive plan to follow. I can either say no altogether, or agree to her terms. And I do want to do this; for the time being, at least.

"OK," I agree.

"Fantastic!" Maybe she's used to time-wasters. I don't know. But it actually makes me feel good, the way she says this, and the way that she smiles. And if I'm to be doing collections, I'll be getting out of town and meeting different people, which is what I wanted. I'm just not used to being turned down.

I follow Jude down the corridor to another office. Tamsin's in there, a computer in front of her, and a haphazard pile of papers. "These are the receipts to say what we've collected, and from whom," she explains. The patronising side of me inwardly congratulates her on her English. "The bigger shops need a paper trail so that they know what's happened to their stock and they can also use these to prove they're fulfilling their *corporate responsibility.*" She emphasises these last two words with a grin and a roll of her eyes. If only she knew just how corporate I've been in my life. No need to find out yet, I think.

Jude says, "Louisa's going to start off doing some of the collections, which will give you more time for data entry."

"That's great," Tamsin smiles at me. "Not the data entry bit, but you doing the collections. And it's true, I could do with more time to collate all this. We're trying to work out who gives us what, and when. We're kind of beholden to them, and it makes it difficult to plan sometimes. Which is why it really is so helpful to have volunteers like you. Sometimes a shop wants something gone, like, immediately, and I might have to drop what I'm doing to go and collect. We don't want to miss out on anything. But we want this place to be as organised as possible. It's a big operation."

"And it's going to get bigger," Jude adds. "If I have my way."

"Oh?" She's piqued my interest. I don't know what I'd expected, but it wasn't this level of organisation, or ambition.

"Yes, I have lots of ideas. *We* do, I should say – sorry, Tamsin."

"That's quite alright!" I admire Tamsin's calm, friendly positivity. Jude is a harder one to work out, but I guess people might say that about me.

"If you stay with us, Louisa," Tamsin smiles at me, "maybe you'll start coming to our meetings, and we can tell you all about our plans."

"In time," Jude says. "Let's see how Louisa likes it first." She's made it sound like it's up to me, but I can tell she really means *let's see how we like Louisa first.* I know her tricks, because I use them. Or used them. It's uncomfortable, being on the receiving end. It's a long time since I really had to prove myself to anyone. And I don't know that I do want to prove myself to Jude. But I feel more comfortable around Tamsin, and if I'm going to be working with her for the majority of the time, then this could work out just fine.

I leave the depot with a couple of dates booked in for next week. Now I have another afternoon to kill. I may as well go and see Mum.

She takes a while to answer the door. I had been on the verge of using my own key – my heart starting to beat a little quicker as I contemplated that this could be it. This could be the day I find her gone. I would never tell Mum that I think like that, of course, and today thankfully I am wrong. I suppose that, having an elderly mum, it's always there, this thought, generally staying just out of reach. Perhaps I've been priming myself for it for years.

But while she is up on her feet, she does not look well. Her face is as pale as I've ever seen it – and she's fair-skinned and strawberry-blonde, so she's not exactly the type to tan much. She looks drawn, and she holds onto the door as she greets me. Nevertheless, she is smiling, and I feel that pang at how much my presence seems to mean to her, and how little I've really appreciated this until recently.

"Mum! Are you OK?"

"Oh yes, just a cold, you know. Probably picked it up at the club. Bill was coughing and sneezing."

Bloody Bill! Why didn't he stay at home if he was ill?

"Have you done a covid test?" I ask her.

"Oh no, I didn't think of that. I don't think it's covid anyway."

"Better to be safe than sorry," I say, thinking that I hope it isn't covid – but I need to put my self-interest aside. I am aware that Mum has not had it yet, while I've had it twice. She's had all the vaccinations she could but even so, at her age I think it poses a real threat to her long-term health. "Come on, you look like you need to sit down. I should have just let myself in, sorry."

I shepherd her back into her living room, where she takes a seat on the settee. Unusual for her – I know she likes to sit near the window, and keep an eye on things. Maybe she doesn't want anyone seeing her looking as she does today. She is visibly relieved to be sitting down.

"You should eat something," I say.

"I'm not all that hungry."

"Have you had breakfast?" I am wary of that turning-of-the-tables thing, of becoming the parent in this situation.

"A little bit of toast and jam," she admits.

"Well, you'll need more than that. Just to keep your blood sugars steady, if nothing else."

"I'll get something in a bit, don't worry."

"I'll sort something out," I say. "And I'll go and grab you a test."

"Aren't you busy?"

"Hardly!" I laugh, and she looks worried. Like maybe she thinks I'm about to flit again, if I'm bored. "But I can tell you about my morning, and what I'll be doing next week."

"That sounds good." She sinks back against the

cushions, and I am struck by how small she looks. The image of a sparrow springs to mind. I sense she's relieved, and for the second time today I feel like I might actually become useful around here. It's not a bad feeling.

First things first, I find the (unopened) box of lateral flow tests in Mum's bathroom cabinet. I take it downstairs and instruct her on how to do it, taking care to stay as far away as I can without being too obvious about it, and also trying not to cast judgement on her for apparently not having done one of these tests before. Sticking the swab up her nose makes her sneeze. I stand back while she squeezes the drops onto the test strip and then I go into the kitchen to make some lunch.

On the work surface is a plate with the remains of a piece of toast and jam, showing clearly that whoever had been eating them was only making a half-hearted effort. I don't say a word, and I'm about to tip them into the bin when I remember Mum's bird table. I tear the toast into small pieces, and I go out into the back garden, tipping the remnants onto it. Almost immediately, a blackbird hops down, a metre or two from my feet.

"Where did you come from?" I ask, then look around to make sure nobody can have heard me talking to a bird. I retreat into the kitchen and root around for a tin of tomato soup, but I keep an eye on the garden via the window above the sink, and I see the blackbird is joined by another, and a couple of sparrows. The remains of Mum's breakfast are soon gone.

While the soup heats, I prepare two cheese sandwiches, slicing Mum's home-made loaf – I'm still impressed that she makes her own – and cutting off the crusts. I hadn't really thought about what I was doing; it's been a long time since I made a sandwich. Ill or not, Mum will not take kindly to being treated like a child.

I pour the soup into two mugs, remembering with a smile when Mum first bought a box of Cup-a-Soup, back in the 1970s. It seemed such a modern and out-there concept. I can almost taste it now, and those little bits of rehydrated dried mushroom.

Putting the sandwiches on small plates, I find a tray for Mum's lunch and take it through to her. Her eyes are closed. I experience a very brief momentary imagining again, of what if she really has died?

Her eyes open, though, and she smiles at me.

I look at the covid test and see that thankfully it is negative. I tell her, as she clearly hasn't bothered to check, and she looks unsurprised, As if Elise Morgan could ever have covid! Then she looks at the tray I am holding and smiles. "Crustless sandwiches, eh? What's this? Afternoon tea at the Ritz?"

"Not quite! I did it without thinking – to mine, too. I suppose I haven't actually made a sandwich in years. I'd make them when Ada was at home."

"But not for yourself?" Mum's eyebrows are raised questioningly.

"No, I..." The truth is, at work somebody would fetch my lunch for me. I can see that is pretty awful. But I was incredibly busy. At home, I might miss lunch altogether, or just grab something ready-made from the fridge. I suppose it was a wasteful way to live. I never really noticed. I could afford it. It was easy. I didn't give it a second thought. But I don't want to tell that to Mum. I feel like she would disapprove.

"Well thank you, Lou, this is really kind of you. But I don't want to keep you from anything."

"Are you trying to get rid of me?"

She laughs, but it sets off a cough, and I take the tray back from her until she's finished. "Certainly not," she manages, eventually.

"Well, maybe I'll stay on for a bit today, if that's alright with you?"

"Of course it is. That would be lovely."

We eat our lunch, and watch something called *Bargain Hunt*. Alright, alright, I've not been that much of a work-addict that I haven't heard of daytime TV before. But I have never watched a whole episode of *Bargain Hunt*. I enjoy it, although I don't think I could make it a regular event.

Mum manages about half the sandwich, and most of the soup. I hope it's not too hot for her. I like it just this side of scalding, and I know she used to, but people change – or their bodies do, at the very least – as they age.

I take her tray from her, and she doesn't even pretend to protest, and I take it through to the kitchen, where I wash up and clean everything. Funny, really, I've never been very much of a domestic, but there's something satisfying in knowing Mum's kitchen is spick and span, and she won't have to bother with anything later.

When I go back through, she has fallen asleep, her mouth ever-so-slightly open. I cover her with a throw that I got her for her last birthday, and then I take her seat, in the window. I can see the appeal of it. Watching the traffic pass by, and pedestrians, blissfully unaware that they are being observed. But then I have a vision of myself in this chair, by the window, and experience a fear of appearing geriatric myself. I hastily get up, checking that I have not disturbed Mum, then I go upstairs to my childhood bedroom.

Laurie and I were fortunate to have our own rooms. We were so lucky to have our own house. I realise this now. As children, you tend to just accept your lot in life, and maybe think it's the same for everyone. Now, I look back at my schoolmates and realise many of them were in rented or social housing. And that won't have changed for today's young families – those who stay in Cornwall. The horror stories in the papers, about towns where nearly 40% of housing stock is now bought up as second homes for out-of-towners. They're not just horror stories, they're true. And while we are still a step behind in this town, in that tourists often pass us by, it's changing all the time. Tied in with the Saltings development – of which I am inextricably a part – there is an element of affordable housing, but by whose standards is it affordable? I've been shocked by what I've seen and heard at the food hub and Pantry, and I am quite sure this is only the tip of the iceberg.

In London, the homelessness problem is visible – or one element of it. The rough-sleepers. The druggies, junkies, alcoholics, the mentally ill. There are so many of them, it comes to seem normal when you pass by these people every day. I don't like it, but I am guilty of having thought that it is not my problem. I suppose I don't want to think too hard about it. Not many people do.

I'm aware that there is another type of homelessness, too, and perhaps that is what I'll be seeing here – if Jude allows me to take on a Front of House role. Young people 'sofa-surfing'; families in temporary, sub-par accommodation, with not enough beds, and no space for the children to do their homework. Struggling to find enough money for breakfasts to start the day the right way. No wonder kids can't concentrate at school. Until recently, I've never given this too much thought. I am not unaware, of course, but it's been just another thing going on in other people's lives. Maybe now it's time that I actually do pay some attention.

Mum has redone my room since I left home, but as that is a good few decades ago, it still feels dated. It is plain, which I like – light blue walls with a couple of pictures by local artists – and the single, metal-framed bed has been replaced at some point, by one made with a fresh, white-painted wood. The duvet is a plain dark blue, and there is a cream rug on the floor. The view from here has not changed much over the years – above the little garden, which Mum extended some time ago by buying the patch of ground beyond our old yard, and across the neighbouring gardens and yards. There's a small alley at the side of our patch, which goes between the houses and onto the street. I used to sneak out that way when I was a teenager. I don't know if Mum ever cottoned on to that or not, but she never mentioned it if she did.

I lie down on the bed, and close my eyes. Try to conjure up those long-ago days. I got stuck somewhere, when Laurie told me about Dad. What he was really like. I had thought my father would have been a good man. Hard-working; maybe absent in the way so many fathers were then, but I had memories – imagined, most probably – of him throwing me up onto his shoulders, holding on tight to my chubby toddler legs as he trotted along like a horse. Me laughing my head off.

Laurie bluntly took the scales from my eyes when it came to our father. And he'd made me promise that I'd be a parent, and he'd be my kids' uncle. He didn't want to risk being a dad like ours had been. But as time had gone on, I'd begun to resent this idea. Why should I be the child-rearer, provider of grandchildren to our mum? When Laurie took off to uni, and from there to one remote island after another, with his bird surveys and his high-minded work, I began to think I'd also like a chance to do my own thing, not to be tied down by children or a partner. I began to work out who I was – and a wife and mother, I was not.

As I lie on the bed and think all this through, I practise John's breathing exercises again. And I realise I have yet to make contact with him, other than an email to let him know I am safely settling in. I mustn't kid myself – he is my therapist, not a friend. And he listens to me because I pay him to. Which is not to say he doesn't care, but it is his job. He sent a kind but brief reply to my email. Boundaries, you know.

As I breathe slowly in and out, I begin to listen. At first to the house, which is not as familiar as you might imagine. There have been changes since I lived here. An updated heating system. A whole new bathroom. The creaky stair I used to listen for as a sign that Mum was going to bed has long since been fixed.

In time, I find the outside sounds, too. The sea is gentle today, and I can just about hear it out there. The gulls, too, sound distant, as my eyes become heavy. I begin to drift in and out of sleep, in waves, not committing either way, fleeting dreams slipping away, just out of reach, until finally I give in.

When I wake, it takes a few moments to realise where I am, and then – Mum! I think of her, and panic. I hurry down the stairs as quietly as I can, and I find that I've only been upstairs for just over an hour, and Mum is still fast asleep on the settee, a slender, shining trail of saliva running from the corner of her mouth like a snail trail. I wipe it gently, not wanting to wake her, but she stirs, but just smiles, her eyes still closed, and slumbers on.

I trawl her bookshelves, settling on *Jamaica Inn*, and I pull one of her cardigans from the back of a chair, shrug it on, then take my book to the window seat, where Mum and I used to read together so many years ago. As her clock ticks steadily and she emits the odd subtle snore, I open the book and begin to read, and I lose myself not only in the world of shipwrecks and wreckers, but back amongst my own childhood years, so many hours spent here in this very spot. My mum close by, always.

2000

She noticed him a long time before they spoke to one another – and it appeared he had noticed her, too.

Louisa's company had created an open-plan office, whereby the majority of employees, no matter what their job title, sat in ranks of desks, separated by felted dividers. These were ideal for drawing pins, enabling people to put up photos of boyfriends, girlfriends, children, football teams, and favourite bands. But this was a habit actively discouraged by the company, which took the line that a tidy desk equals a tidy mind. Louisa approved.

Still, there were a handful of offices reserved for the absolute upper echelons, including the man now striding purposefully along the lane next to Louisa's desk. Since he had come over from America, she had almost immediately become familiar with his size, and his shape, just in terms of his outline as he emerged from the lift. He was tall, with short, greying hair, which seemed always to have just been cut, and his suits looked expensive. He exuded confidence, and when he spoke, people listened, sometimes laughing nervously if they were unsure of his humour. But Louisa got him. She was sure of it. In meetings, of which there were many, he was self-assured but sparing of words. She liked that.

Some of her colleagues (97.5% male) she had known since her early twenties, and they were heading together into their forties. The majority had married and supposedly settled down in this time, yet flirted outrageously with the younger female support staff, forgetting their girlfriends, their wives, and their children (maybe if they'd been allowed to put up pictures this wouldn't have happened, although Louisa doubted anything would stop them trying to have it all), entertaining clients an excuse for visiting strip clubs and putting it on expenses. They were competitive, and despite the apparent camaraderie, she had no doubt that they would gladly stamp on another's hand if he was hanging over the cliff, or step on his head if it meant getting a little further up in the company hierarchy.

She had quickly been written off as boring, and uptight, and certainly no good for a quick, illicit shag in the toilets. Louisa kept her head down, and her hems long, but she knew that to a certain type of man this was not unattractive. And this certain type of man had recently arrived in the office, and very regularly would walk past her desk, his eyes meeting hers as he approached. There was never a smile, nor a word of greeting, but Louisa was sure that there was an unspoken, mutual understanding between the two of them.

It was only at the Christmas party that this was proved correct, when he appeared by her side as she was carefully selecting four small sandwiches and some cherry tomatoes. This little buffet was a precursor, she knew, to a far wilder night, but she would not be invited to the later goings-on, and nor did she wish to be.

"Steady on there," a deep voice came from just behind her right shoulder. "Leave something for the rest of us."

She turned, startled, to see him smiling at her. A glance at her meagre pickings, then at the huge table overladen with platters and bowls confirmed he was joking. She smiled back.

"I'm so sorry, what was I thinking?"

He took a pile of sandwiches and a handful of crisps. "Mind if I join you?"

"Erm, no. Of course."

"If you're not already taken," he said.

"Hardly!" Louisa suppressed a snort. He clearly had little idea of the social side of the office. "I mean, no, that would be nice."

She led the way across to a small table, knowing full well that the eyes of all the office would be on him and her. Louisa Morgan, who barely spoke to anyone, and never socialised. She knew what they'd say about her. Hobnobbing with the big boss. Trying to sleep her way to the top. She'd long since stopped caring about all that, though. Not since she was a junior, in her early twenties, and realising that this world was a tough one, especially for a woman. It hadn't put her off. Conversely, it had made her all the more determined. She was going to go all the way to the top, but it wouldn't be from sleeping with anyone, and it wouldn't be from flirting or fluttering her eyelashes, or wearing short, tight skirts. Louisa realised thinking like that made her an enemy of her female colleagues as much as the men, but she wasn't a sisterhood kind of person. She just wanted to see what she could do. And she was sure she could do a lot. She didn't need a man to open doors for her, literally or metaphorically.

Nevertheless, Gianni Capaldi, with his cool blue eyes and his Italian-American New York accent, was following her across the room, seemingly unfazed by any thought of what this might look like to his London office.

"It kills me, what you Brits think is a sandwich!" he said, dropping a square of white bread filled with cheese and pickle into his mouth and appearing to swallow it whole. "You oughta see a New York sandwich. You'll never look back. Ever been to New York?"

"No, not yet. I'd like to," Louisa said politely, also thinking she might as well mention that. Maybe she'd be seconded to the office there sometime. Perhaps there things would be different. More women, more equality. America was far ahead of UK in so many ways. "I love American writers," she continued. "I've wanted to see America since I was a kid."

"Is that so?" he smiled at her. "And are you from London?"

"No, I'm from Cornwall. In the south-west." She didn't know if he'd have heard of it.

"Oh yes, the Riviera. I've been told I should go there."

Louisa's mind flew back across the years to her first trip to London. The marketing Elise had identified had clearly paid off.

"I don't know if Riviera is a bit grand for it, to be honest. I think we've got the tourist office to thank for that."

"Well, maybe you can give me some pointers. Maybe even show me around."

"And you can show me New York!" She had no idea where that boldness had come from, but it made him laugh. Which sent some of her colleagues' heads turning their way, briefly, then turning back together for some muttering, no doubt cursing her, and casting aspersions on her good name.

Gianni was soon commandeered by Gerald Lacey, who swept him away with a cursory nod to Louisa, and she was left to eat her sandwiches and tomatoes alone. She cleared away her plate, grabbed her bag and coat, and made a sharp exit before the evening took a turn for the worse. Would Gianni be joining them for their night on the tiles? She hoped not. And surely he would keep some kind of distance between himself and his underlings, but who could tell? He was a man, after all.

On the Monday, she was disappointed to discover he'd flown back to the States, and would not be in London again until the new year. She went to Cornwall for Christmas, but was back at work on the day after Boxing Day, leaving Elise feeling like she had barely seen her daughter. Not that she would say anything to that effect.

On New Year's Eve, Louisa was working late, trying to get ahead while the city partied around her. She liked the office when it was empty. The orderly lines of desks, the computer screens blank, the screens and keyboards polished by attentive cleaners. The pleasing scent of anti-bacterial spray. The lights were on low, and outside were streets of other buildings, some in darkness, others lit up – many decorated for Christmas and the holidays. Louisa could walk back to her house from the office; it would take forty minutes or so, but she didn't mind. The streets would be busy tonight, and when she was home she would congratulate herself with a glass of the champagne that was chilling in the fridge. She had awarded herself a full day off for New Year's Day, and the thought of an incredibly rare lie-in was appealing. Maybe a walk on the heath later in the day – but maybe a lazy day in pyjamas, watching whatever films were on. She wouldn't do it. She couldn't. Not get dressed? Only if she was ill – which she never was.

Her mind deep in the figures on her spreadsheet, it took her a moment to realise that the sound of the lift doors opening was unexpected at this time of night, particularly on this night. She looked up, confused, her head still full of numbers.

It was Gianni.

"Louisa!" he said. She hadn't realised he knew her name. "Why the hell are you at work on New Year's Eve?"

"I could ask you the same thing."

"Sure. But in New York, it's still morning."

"But you're not in New York."

She felt emboldened around him somehow, and all the more so in the soft, dim lighting, with nobody else around except the security guard downstairs.

He just laughed. "True. Haven't you anywhere better to be, though? Family? Friends? Boyfriend?"

"Not really. My mum's in Cornwall, my brother's on some remote island counting puffins or something, my friends are married with kids, and... no boyfriend."

"Even so..."

"It's just another night. And I like the quiet. Plus, the view of the fireworks at midnight is spectacular."

"You've done this before, then?"

"Once or twice." Every single year.

"Well, I'd better..." he gestured towards his office with his briefcase.

"Of course. Me too." She looked back at her screen.

"See you later," he said.

Louisa suppressed a smile as he walked away. She would not have envisaged being able to make Gianni Capaldi feel awkward.

She saw the light go on in his office, but the blinds

were down, which was probably a good thing, really. She could do without the distraction.

It was nearly half past eleven when he emerged.

"You're still here!" He looked pleased.

"I am."

"For the fireworks?" he asked.

"Well, I suppose I might as well, seeing as it's nearly midnight."

"Mind if I join you?"

She thought of how he had asked that same thing at the Christmas party. Was he the kind of man who expected never to be refused?

"Of course. I mean, I don't mind at all."

"Are you always so polite?"

"I am, actually."

That made him laugh out loud, and Louisa felt a rush of pleasure.

"Well, can I offer you a drink? I've got some whisky from duty-free."

"That sounds nice. Thank you."

"Come on, then."

"I'll just turn my computer off."

"Sure."

She'd thought he'd go, but he stood and waited, and then he walked with her towards his office, standing back to let her go in first.

Would he close the door? She felt suddenly very aware that she was alone with this man; a virtual stranger. To her relief – and embarrassingly also a slight tinge of disappointment – he left the door open. He scooped a couple of glasses from a tray, and pulled a bottle of whisky from a thick, strong carrier bag. A surreptitious glance at his hand confirmed there was no wedding ring there, and a further subtle investigation revealed no pictures of a wife or children. He was surely free to decorate his office how he pleased, but there was just a potted plant, and a large, framed photograph of the New York skyline at night.

"Cheers." He handed her a glass, knocking his gently against it.

"Cheers." They both took a sip, and she inhaled sharply, then started coughing.

"Not a whisky drinker, huh?" he laughed.

"Is it that obvious?" she said, still spluttering, and red-faced.

He patted her on the back, then rubbed in between her shoulder blades. "You should have said."

"You're right, I should. I don't know why I didn't."

"Can I get you something else? Some water?"

"Water would be great. Thank you."

She stood looking out of his window at the lights of the city. Gianni returned with a mug. "Sorry I couldn't find any glasses."

"That's absolutely fine."

"There she goes with the politeness again." He bumped his arm gently, teasingly, against hers.

"That's me."

He sipped his whisky contemplatively while Louisa cradled her mug of water.

"I've had worse New Years," he said.

"Me too."

As the sky exploded with colour, Gianni wished Louisa a Happy New Year, and offered her a chaste kiss on the cheek. "I hope that was ok," he said.

"Now who's the polite one?"

"I don't want you thinking I'm taking advantage. You work for my company, and you're a young, attractive woman. I shouldn't even be saying that to you."

"I've heard worse," Louisa smiled at him.

"Still. It isn't really acceptable, is it?"

"It's fine."

As the fireworks subsided, Gianni pulled on his jacket. "Come on, Ms Morgan. You need to get home. Let me get you a cab."

"Thank you," she said, again feeling ever so slightly disappointed.

They were quiet in the lift, both more than aware of the other's proximity. As the doors opened on the ground floor, he let her step out first, then they both wished the security guard a Happy New Year.

"Hope it's a good one, Paul," Gianni said, and Louisa felt ashamed that she hadn't known Paul's name. It slipped easily from Gianni's tongue.

He hailed a taxi, like this was New York, and pressed a £20 note into her hand. "Goodnight, Louisa." He smiled before closing the car door and banging lightly on the side to send her on her way.

Louisa sat back, realising she was smiling. Something told her it was going to be a good year.

Louisa

Although Mum starts to recover, the bug has really knocked her, and she looks a little bit older and frailer. I just hope that she gets back to her normal strong self soon. In the meantime, I've landed myself with a bit of a situation. Maggie's mum, Lucy, is moving down this weekend, and Mum had agreed to look after Stevie while Maggie drove up and collected some of Lucy's belongings. Now, of course, Mum isn't up to it, and when she asked me if I could have Stevie, I had no ready excuse not to.

I don't mind, really. She's a nice girl, and seems quite easy. I do wish Ada was here, though, to help out. I was an older mum for her (still am), and I'm old enough to be Stevie's grandmother. Still, I've said I will do it, and I suppose Stevie is old enough to entertain herself a lot of the time. As long as I don't end up having to watch all those bloody TikToks again.

Another effect of Mum being ill was equally unexpected. I ended up staying over for two nights, as I really didn't feel comfortable leaving her to fend for herself. The first night, she became very hot, and I was contemplating ringing for a doctor, or taking her to A&E or something, but she begged me not to. I gave her some paracetamol and monitored her, and her temperature did start to come down, but she was drifting in and out of consciousness – and of herself, it seemed to me.

"Maudie," she said at one point, calling me by the name of her old friend. They met at work, and Maudie was a part of our lives for as long as I can remember – although Laurie tells me Dad didn't like her. She died a few years ago, and I know Mum has missed her terribly. Again, I experience a pang of guilt that I wasn't more present, all the more so during the covid lockdowns when Mum coped admirably well on her own, but I was as stuck as she was, really. I couldn't leave London, and I was scared of what I might bring with me to this far-off corner of the land. Besides, I still had to work, and keep things going, even if I couldn't get into the office. Mum said she understood.

Nevertheless, I should have been more thoughtful when it came to Maudie. I stupidly assumed the loss of a friend at this age would not be so painful because surely it is to be expected.

"It's alright," I said, and I pressed a cool, damp flannel to her forehead.

Then her eyes sprung open. "Louisa!" she exclaimed, as though surprised.

"It's OK, Mum."

"Are you alright?"

"I'm fine," I soothed.

"And AJ?"

"AJ's fine." His name had given me a shock, but I quickly smoothed over it. Mum was the important one here.

"I know all about it."

"It's OK, Mum. We'll talk about it later." I didn't know

what else to say. Had Tony been talking to Maggie, and she in turn to Mum? Or was it just Mum's fever talking?

"You're a good girl." She smiled and closed her eyes, and returned to her slumber, but her words niggled at me, reawakening unwelcome thoughts and feelings.

In the morning, Mum seemed brighter, and she hasn't mentioned AJ since – consequently, neither have I. She did, however, ask me about Stevie. So here I am, bright and early on a Saturday morning, waiting on the harbourside for Maggie to drop off her progeny.

"Hi Louisa!" I see her coming towards me, waving and smiling. Stevie is a little more reticent, although she also smiles at me, and I feel myself relax a little.

"How's Elise?" Maggie asks. I find I am glad to be able to impart news of my mother to her. She may be Maggie's friend, but she is my mother, after all.

"Thank you so much for doing this." Maggie looks at me with a slight edge of worry. "It's not too late for Stevie to come with me, you know, if we're keeping you from anything. It's just that I wouldn't be able to get so much in the car and I'd have to make two trips and…"

"It's fine," I reassure her. "More than fine," I say, smiling at Stevie. "I'm looking forward to it."

"Well thank you," Maggie still looks doubtful. "Can I give you some money to get some lunch, though? For both of you, I mean? I should be able to collect her before tea-time."

"No, I won't hear of it. Honestly, we can make ourselves something, or maybe pop down to the café… what do you think, Stevie?"

"I don't mind, whatever's best for you," she says so

politely that any last traces of my ambivalence about today dissolve.

"Maybe we can call Ada too," I suggest. "She'll be coming for a visit soon, and I know she's looking forward to seeing you."

"I hope you don't mind," Maggie says, "but Stevie's got some homework in her bag as well. In case you run out of things to do!"

"All sounds great," I say briskly. Business-like once more. "Now you get on your way, and we can go upstairs, Stevie. You can tell me what homework you've got."

"Thank you." Maggie's smile is wide and genuine, and her dimples make her look even younger than she really is. "Be good, Stevie, OK?"

"Yes, Mum." I can feel the nearly-teenage impatience in Stevie, and easily remember Ada being like this.

We take the lift up to my floor, and Stevie steps out to admire the view from the hallway window. Although it's not possible to see the sea, we can look across the town from above, and beyond to the farmland and the moors not all that far away.

"Wow!"

"Not bad, eh?"

"It's amazing!" She presses her nose to the glass.

"Come on in, I'll show you around."

There are two doors on this floor – one to my apartment, and one to Stacey's. I am slightly ashamed to say that I generally check through my peephole before exiting the flat, to make sure she's not on her way in or out. I also have become adept at listening for sounds of the family.

The boys seem to be out a lot of the time, and Stacey

has told me it's because they are doing martial arts/swimming/surfing/boxing/basketball (delete as applicable). "I used to do a lot when I was young. Gym, swimming, dance. Mum always took me, and I loved it. Being at home was too quiet. We did have pets. I liked that. But I really wanted a brother or sister." That confession managed to provoke a little sympathy in me. But she quickly extinguished it: "So now the boys get to do everything they want. They're good at everything, too. Top of the class at school, and fighting it out for top place in all their clubs. Sometimes actually fighting!"

She had laughed, and I'd inwardly grimaced. I am all too familiar with this kind of parent, although at least Stacey is open about her vicarious pride. I struggled when Ada was at school. Being by far the oldest parent in the playground, I was quickly disabused of my notion that I would work part-time, to be there for Ada. I did want to be there for her, but I couldn't bear the playground conversations; the humble bragging over children's achievements. The endless criticism of the school and the teachers.

Refusing to be drawn in, and no doubt appearing offhand and aloof, I had been side-lined very quickly by the young, trendy mummies.

I'd stand next to the occasional father, and make awkward conversation. I was a fish out of water – so confident at work, yet so full of doubt in this world of soft play parties, and swimming lessons, music lessons, football training and 'play dates'. Wasn't that just having someone round to play? Mum was good at that, and we often had friends at our house, although more often than not we'd be out rather than in, down on the harbour or one of the beaches. And no, I am not one of those people who lament that supposedly perfect life when children were out all day and only came back at mealtimes. There were good things and bad things when I was growing up, just as there are today.

I hear the sound of the lock being freed on Stacey's door, and out they come – all five of them today – before I have had a chance to shepherd Stevie into my place.

"Oh hi, Louise," Stacey says, barely looking at Stevie. The boys troop out after her, all looking at their phones and not even noticing us. Eventually comes Sean, the husband. His eyes fall on Stevie, almost quizzically. Is he wondering if she's my daughter? No, I imagine he'll be thinking more like granddaughter. I find I want to tell him I'm looking after her for a friend – but why? What does it matter what he thinks?

"Hello," Stevie says to him in her open, friendly manner. What a lovely girl she is. Maggie must be very proud.

"Hi." And that's it. He barely even looks at me. He's not very chatty but then, being married to Stacey, he probably doesn't get much of a chance to be.

"Going somewhere nice?" I ask.

"Judo tournament!" Stacey beams. "I'll let you know how they get on."

"Lovely."

The five of them get into the lift. To give him his due, Sean does turn and smile then, just before the doors close. When he smiles, he reminds me of somebody, but I can't quite place who it is.

Having Stevie around is a pleasure. And it all feels very familiar. Very teenage. Not that she is moody – she is quite delightful. I find myself hoping that she at least gives her mum a hard time at home. Nobody deserves to get away with having a completely angelic teenager. But then I remember people saying similar things to me about Ada. I suppose she and Stevie share a similar background, with relatively quiet, grown-up lives, each with just a mum for company, and no siblings to compete with. Possibly it means they have less reason to be spiky.

We spend the morning working on her homework (maths), and using my binoculars to watch the seabirds and look for seals (we spot one) and dolphins (none, but I know they don't come this close to town – Stevie seems to be enjoying keeping her eye out for them anyway). Then we go to the café for lunch. She has a strawberry milkshake and a five-cheese toastie. Five cheese! I can only dream. I can't allow myself to eat things like that these days. I do, however, find myself ordering a vegetarian option – houmous and roasted vegetables in a wrap – because Stevie is vegetarian. I even try a flat white with oat milk, and it's quite acceptable.

After lunch, at Stevie's request, we walk round to Mum's, stopping to pick up some Dairy Milk and flowers for her. I text Mum to let her know we are going to 'surprise' her, just in case she's asleep, or in a state of undress. She sends me a thumbs-up back (she knows her way around a phone) and does a great job of appearing surprised when we arrive on her doorstep. She is so happy that Stevie has thought of her, and we go inside for a cup of tea. I make it while Stevie and Mum chat away like old friends, which I suppose they are.

We don't stay too long, but I promise Mum I'll be back tomorrow. Our next stop is across the road and down to the beach. There is a touch of winter to the air today – a little forewarning of what is to come – and the beach seems a little duller, with a thick line of seaweed and scattered pieces of driftwood deposited by the sea. I mimic Maggie's trick, discarding about fifty per cent of the stones, shells and other bits of detritus that Stevie hands me as she runs up and down to the shore and back. She is delighted to find a small Lego figure, and I know I must hold on to him, even though his face has been made blank by the sea.

Following our walk, it's back to mine for a film. Stevie recommends we watch *Inside Out* and to my shame I find I shed a few tears, when Riley is growing up.

Stevie looks at me. "Mum always cries at that bit, too." She smiles, and I laugh.

Shortly after the film, there is a text from Maggie, to say she's on her way, with Lucy.

"Your mum will be here soon," I tell Stevie.

"I know, I got a message too." She waves her phone at me.

"Of course."

And I feel a little bit regretful that the day is almost at a close. It's been good, having a youngster around – and feeling busy, and useful, and wanted – again.

2001

It didn't happen immediately, but Louisa knew that it was inevitable. The looks between them grew more intense, and she was sure that the others would notice, but nobody seemed to. Exchanges between them were cursory, perfunctory, and Louisa kept her head down, working hard, as she always did. It was just that when Gianni was in the office, it was a tiny bit harder to concentrate.

It wasn't until April that he kissed her, properly. Circumstances had them both working late again, just the two of them. The year had turned, and the sky was light until well after eight, but by the time she was shutting down her computer, darkness had settled in. She was just putting her bag over her shoulder when she saw his office door open.

"Louisa! You're still here!"

"I'm just about to go, actually." Did that sound rude? Like she was trying to get away?

"Me too." If she had sounded rude, it appeared not to have bothered him. "I'm going to grab something to eat. Care to join me?"

"Oh, erm, yes, that would be good."

"Great."

They walked together, side by side, but maintaining a professional distance, dodging between the various other people who were milling about. Other late-night workers, tourists, theatre-goers.

"Do you have somewhere in mind?" Louisa asked.

"Not really, no. I just assume we'll find somewhere good soon. This is London, after all."

"I know somewhere. An Italian, actually," she smiled.

"Oh good. The taste of home."

She looked to see if he was being sarcastic, but he was looking at her and grinning.

"Like Mama used to make?" she suggested.

"Exactly."

Bocca Felice. Happy mouth. The very same restaurant where she had eaten with Elise, so many years before, and where she returned every now and then, when she was in need of something like home comfort. She had never told Elise this, for some reason, although she knew that her mum would be pleased to think of it. The original proprietor was old now, his son and daughter-in-law running the place. Tonight, the old man was sitting at the bar.

"Ciao!" he greeted her.

"Ciao." She smiled. She could sense Gianni's eyes on her, and felt her face flushing. "May we have a table for two?"

"Wherever you like."

Louisa led the way to a table tucked away from the window. It would be entirely typical for one of her colleagues to see her dining out with the big boss.

It seemed Gianni appreciated this, too. "Smart thinking."

A woman brought across the menus, then a bowl of olives and some breadsticks. For some reason, Louisa found herself telling Gianni about coming here with her mum and them not touching the breadsticks.

He laughed. "I wouldn't have known what to do, either."

"Really?"

"Really. We never ate out when I was a kid. Couldn't

afford to. Not that I'm getting the sympathy violins out."

"So you're a real product of the American dream?"

"I guess I am." He smiled at her, his eyes finding hers and holding her gaze for just a moment longer than felt entirely respectable for an employer and employee.

"I didn't mean to sound sarcastic."

"Hey, you're a Brit, aren't you meant to be sarcastic?"

"I suppose I am."

That laugh again – the full, guileless, genuine amusement. She tried not to look too pleased with herself.

They ordered pasta and caprese salad, and a bottle of red – and then another. Discussing tales from their childhoods, and the neighbourhoods they had grown up in. Louisa's so different to his.

They stayed long after the other diners had left, and Louisa shivered as they stepped into the cool night air. Gianni pulled his jacket around her shoulders. "I mean it, I want you to show me Cornwall," he said.

"Sure. I mean, I would gladly, but wouldn't that be…"

"Inappropriate?" he asked, then he kissed her. He had his arm around her waist, and he pulled her in towards him. She had never been kissed quite like this before. Or she had never felt quite like this when she had been kissed before.

"I hope that's OK," he said as he took a step back.

"It's absolutely fine," she said, and he laughed, as she had known he would.

"Could I ask you back to my hotel room?"

"Yes, you could ask."

"And would you say yes?"

"I think I probably would."

At work the next day, Louisa felt like all eyes were on her. As though it must be obvious. But nobody spoke to her any differently, or treated her with any more or less attention than they would normally. She went about her usual routine and when Gianni passed by, he didn't greet her. She tried not to let it bother her. He wouldn't, would he? He couldn't treat her any differently.

Then she saw him leaving in the mid-afternoon, and Teresa, Gerald Lacey's PA, caught up with him to tell him a flight number. So he was really going. Louisa's stomach dropped, and she felt like a fool. What had she expected, though? He was the managing director, and she was a senior executive. A title which felt entirely empty.

She turned back to her screen to see she had a little mail icon. Her heart skipped a beat when she saw the name, and the subject line.

G. Capaldi: Urgent

She cast a surreptitious glance left and right before opening the email.

Yesterday's meeting was extremely productive and has given me much to think about. Today, duty calls and I need to get back to the US but we should catch up next week.

Yours,

Gianni

It said so little, and yet so much. She had to read it and re-read it three times, then think about it before responding. Was he saying what she thought he was saying? She kept her reply brief.

Dear Gianni,

Thank you for your email. I hope you have a safe and successful trip to the States. I would be glad to catch up when you return.

With kind regards,

Louisa

She couldn't help smiling as she sent it. And then immediately she worried that she had phrased things wrong, and she hoped that she had correctly understood his meaning, and conveyed her own, correctly. She had to read his email again, and then her sent reply, for reassurance. And then she deleted both, and told herself to stop being ridiculous.

It became the norm, when Gianni was in town, for them to eat together – often at Bocca Felice, at what Gianni came to call their table, and sometimes in his hotel room, wrapped in sheets, feeding each other from the room service tray. He never came to her house, and she never invited him, although she wasn't sure why not. Perhaps just because of the nature of their relationship. It was good, it was beautiful, and exciting, and she knew he really liked her. But she knew it could not go on. Or at least not in the same vein. She would have to leave the company, and she had worked very hard to get where she was – and she knew where she wanted to go. Nevertheless, she began to keep her eyes open for other opportunities. She even stopped ignoring calls from recruitment agents – some of them, at least.

She was allowing a relationship to make her take her eye off the ball. Something she had sworn she would never do. But he made her feel something she hadn't felt in a long time. Happy. And good about herself. And excited about life.

During phone calls, Elise picked up on the change in her daughter's voice, but Louisa wasn't giving anything away.

"Everything alright, Lou?" her mum would ask.

"Yes thanks, Mum." Louisa remained tight-lipped. Perhaps because her mum might say what she already knew. That an affair with her boss was unlikely to end well.

And Elise would have been right, if she had known about Gianni, and had the chance to offer such advice. But it wasn't for the reason she may have thought.

In September 2001, Gianni flew back out to the States for work. Louisa had stayed over in his hotel room the night before, and they'd kissed in the early morning. He'd ordered breakfast for her, before heading into the office himself. She had followed an hour or two later. As always, he left in the mid-afternoon, passing her desk but saying nothing.

As he got in the lift, she dared a look across at him, and their eyes met just before the lift doors closed.

He emailed her when he arrived in New York, from his personal email address to hers.

To: LAM_1957@yahoo.com
From: Gcap@hotmail.com
Date: 09/10/2001
Time: 18:56

Counting the days till I'm back in LDN. Gx

She wondered what his home was like. Whether she might go out and visit him there. These idle thoughts drifted through her tired mind, and in the morning she got up, got dressed, and went into work, as she did any other day.

She worked through lunch. Now more than ever, she was determined that any success she might experience would be indisputably earned. Imagine if it should get out – as it very possibly, or even probably, would at some point – about her and Gianni. Certainly, if they made it 'official', then people would know. She could not have anyone thinking that she was reliant on her boyfriend for any pay rises or promotions that came her way.

Not long after lunch, Carlos came bowling into the office. "Have you heard?" he exclaimed.

"Heard what?" Steve, at the next desk to Louisa, asked.

"What's happening in New York. A plane's flown into the World Trade Center."

At the name 'New York', Louisa's ears had pricked up. But she remained intent on her screen, merely listening. Carlos was renowned for being a bit over-the-top about things. And yet, just minutes later, he exclaimed. "Fuck!"

"What?" She turned this time, answering sharply.

"Another one. Another plane."

Louisa opened an internet browser. She looked for the BBC website. And there it was – something far more disastrous and dramatic than she could ever have imagined. Two planes – not small, light aircraft, but full-sized passenger planes – had flown into the Twin Towers.

"Shit!"

"Told you!" said Carlos.

They gathered around Louisa's computer screen, watching in horror as the story unfolded. She was desperate to contact Gianni, who, although he didn't work at the World Trade Center, would almost certainly know people who did, and would no doubt be in shock at what was happening to his city.

"Let's put it on in the conference room, shall we?" Steve asked, and Louisa was grateful. As the others filed away, she said, "I'll be there in a moment." Nobody heard her or noticed anyway. But she took the chance to send a quick personal email to Gianni:

To: Gcap@hotmail.com
From: LAM_1957@yahoo.com
Date: 11/09/2001
Time: 15:08

I can't believe it! I really hope you are OK and all your friends and family. How utterly shocking. I don't know what else to say. Lxx

She wasn't normally one for putting kisses at the end of messages, but it was an emotional day. An unbelievable day. She joined her colleagues in the conference room, for once glad of their presence as they all sat in shock, mostly in silence, aside from the occasional exclamation to punctuate the quiet.

People falling – if not willingly, then by choice (what pitiful choice they had), from windows so many storeys up, just to escape the horrors within.

And it was all that was on TV – who could think about anything else, anyway? – all afternoon and through the evening, overnight and into the next day.

Louisa walked home, as many did that night, the autumn air soothing against their skin, and the presence of other humans, unknown but so solidly there, a comfort on this most shocking of days.

She showered and put pyjamas on, and turned on her laptop, checking intermittently for an email from Gianni, but presumably there would be problems with the internet, and god knew what else going on over there.

Drinking nearly a bottle of wine made no dent on her alertness and it was hours before she fell into a light, restless sleep.

In the morning, it was still all anyone was talking about, on the TV, on the radio. She turned them off. Louisa got ready for work in silence. What more could she possibly need to know? On autopilot, she showered, dressed, and went into work. There were a handful of others in already, offering weak smiles of greeting and looking drawn and grey-skinned.

At 9am, Gerald Lacey called the senior executive team in for a meeting. Louisa filed in with the others.

"Team," he said, clearing his throat. He too looked

tired and pale. "You will all be aware of the shocking events in New York and Washington. It is my terribly sad duty to tell you that we ourselves have been touched directly by this."

His audience cast quick, worried and puzzled glances towards each other.

"I'm sorry to say that our managing director, Gianni Capaldi, was caught up in the events of yesterday. At the World Trade Center, I mean." He cleared his throat.

There was a collective gasp. Louisa felt like she had been punched in the stomach.

"But we don't have offices in the Twin Towers," Carlos said.

"No, no, quite correct, Carlos. Gianni was there for a meeting. By all accounts, he'd only just arrived, when it happened. I'm sorry to say that he's missing, presumed dead."

Louisa felt as though all of the air had been sucked out of the room, and then her vision turned dark, and she felt herself falling through merciful blackness.

Louisa

Aside from a minor run-in with Jude, my first week helping out at the food hub is satisfactory. Three days out of five, I am dispatched to various supermarkets and smaller retailers, to collect trays of vegetables, fruit, bread, and tins close to their sell-by dates. I bring them back to the depot, where three volunteers, all men in their sixties – John, Matthew and Mark (where is Luke, I wonder?) – insist on carrying everything in. Even though I am quite capable of doing it myself. I can see they just want to help, though, and I suppose they would feel bad if they stood back and watched me doing all the heavy lifting.

"Tell you what," John says, "I'd kill for a cuppa. Why don't you put the kettle on, Louisa, while we're shifting this stuff?"

I bristle, but remind myself this is a different kind of place to where I used to work. And maybe it's not such an unreasonable request. I smile through gritted teeth. "Sure. What are you drinking?"

"Three white teas, one with sugar, for Mark. I'm sweet enough." John laughs at his own joke.

I smile again, but this time it's not so forced. It's alright, I tell myself. We are all volunteers, and they are doing me a favour, so I am sure I can make them a cup of tea in return. We are not in competition here; we are all part of the same team.

On my first day, I had wandered into the building, where there were another six or seven volunteers working alongside Tamsin, sorting and packing the trays ready for delivery. They all smiled or offered a hello but, as they were all clearly intent on their work, I felt a bit lost.

"Can I help with this?" I asked.

Tamsin looked up and smiled. "Oh no, that's fine, thank you. I think we've got it all sorted."

"Like a well-oiled machine," I said, and she smiled again but clearly her mind was on the task at hand.

I know I've said it already, but being a newcomer is a truly odd feeling. I'm used to being consulted about, well, almost everything – and being instrumental to the running of multi-million-pound projects. Now I'm surplus to requirements at a small food hub. But I don't mean to belittle it, or what they do. It's just that the comparison is difficult to get my head around.

I excused myself to go to the ladies, avoiding my reflection in the cracked mirror. The sole cubicle was busy, and I waited for the flush, then Jude emerged.

"Hi Louisa! Back already?"

"Oh! Yes, it didn't take that long, actually. And I'm not allowed to carry the trays in!" I laughed.

"Ah yes, I'm afraid that the age of chivalry lives on here." Washing her hands, she looked at me via that cracked mirror. "But it is meant in the best way."

"I realise that." My words came out more sharply than I had expected.

"I know you're used to being top of the tree at work, but we all try to help each other out around here. In whatever way we can. I aim to keep things as equal as possible."

The conversation for some reason had taken an abrupt, frostier turn and I'm not sure quite why or how. I suppose I've given Jude a particular impression of myself.

I did my best to rectify it, but I couldn't quite fight the stiffness in my delivery. "I realise that," I said again, and – keen not to sound so cold – I added, "And I admire it, too."

"Bit different to your corporate offices, though?"

"Well, yes, but that's not necessarily a bad thing."

"Not necessarily? Not at all."

"Alright, I agree. But there's space for everything in this world, don't you think?"

"Well, no, I don't, actually, but we can agree to differ, can't we?" Her manner changed as she seemed to remind herself of her position and mine. Here, she is 'top of the tree', as she put it. I am just a volunteer.

"Of course we can," I said smoothly. "But I was meaning to ask if you're applying for one of the grants, from Canyon, I mean?"

"Yes, of course, we apply for everything we can get."

"So you don't mind accepting help from them?"

"Well, no. I don't. As they're part of the problem, I am more than happy to take what I can from them."

"Making them part of the solution?"

"No. That's not it at all. While I appreciate the possibility of some funding, it should not be necessary in the first place. Thanks to the nature of the world we live in, where profit is king, we are seeing more and more clients coming in."

"Clients? That makes it sound like this is a business."

She actually smiled genuinely then, taking me by surprise. "You're right. I personally hate that word. I don't know what else to call them, though. 'Service users' makes them sound like drug addicts. 'Customers' makes it sound like they are paying. If you've got any ideas, let me know."

I admired the way she was able to quickly defuse the escalating antipathy between us. In another world, she and I might get on. But we don't live in another world.

"I'll think on it. And I did want to say, if you need a hand with funding applications, I'd be more than happy to help. I might be an asset, having some insider insight."

"Thank you, Louisa. And I should apologise, for launching into one of my lectures. I just feel very passionate about this place. And about our... clients... for want of a better word." She had smiled again, slightly bashfully, and her blue eyes seemed to soften a little, as she looked at me.

"I can tell you are. And I would think you need to be, to make this place work. Honestly, Jude, I'm not here for anything other than to help. And I might have knowledge that could be useful to you. So use me!"

"I might just do that. And thank you, Louisa. Your time and help are greatly appreciated, even if it may not have sounded like it just now!"

I left that first day feeling surprisingly buoyed up, although both subsequent visits have left me twiddling my thumbs a little. It seems that at the moment I am only being trusted to collect, and nothing more. But I am finding myself increasingly interested in the way the place runs, and what kind of things the 'clients' need. I am also aware that there is a lot of funding out there, from the greedy corporates (as Jude thinks of them) needing to wash their dirty hands in the name of social responsibility.

Nevertheless, even though I have only done a handful of hours, I am still able to feel pleased at the approach of the weekend. I have nothing definite planned, but I'm happy to have some free days, and see what I fancy. I might pop to the cinema one evening. I don't mind going alone. Lots of people do, in London. I wonder if it's the same here?

I will also go and see Mum. I've dropped by most days this week and she's making slow progress towards full health again, but that illness has really knocked her, and left her with a horrible, racking cough, which is in itself exhausting.

I decide to treat myself, and Mum, to some M&S food, and after leaving the hub on Friday lunchtime, I drive just out of town to the little retail park. There's a Next there, too, and I find myself wandering in and looking at jeans. Not the skinny, designer jeans I am used to, but the more casual type. Like Tamsin, and Jude, wear. Could I get away with them? Would I want to? I find myself wondering what Jude will think. Picking up two pairs – one black, one grey – I decide to take them home to try on. On my way to the till, I spot some trainers as well. I do have trainers, but they're an expensive pair meant for exercising, bought from one of those posh shops where they check your gait and make sure you pay the full price of having flat feet. These trainers are more casual, and have pretty much no arch support whatsoever. I pick up a plain black pair in my size, and I go to pay for them. While I am standing in the queue, I hear a voice behind me.

"Louise?"

It takes me a moment to realise that it's me who is being addressed. I turn, already knowing who it will be. And there she is, her arms laden with clothes – not all for her, I note; some boys' shirts and trousers are mixed in amongst shiny, glittering dresses and tops.

"Oh, hi Stacey," I say. "Going somewhere nice?" I indicate the clothes.

"What? No... well, actually, I'm glad I bumped into you. We're having a little housewarming – Sean and the boys and myself."

"Oh, lovely, that sounds good. Maybe I should think about doing something similar." I don't know what I'm talking about. And who would I invite? Mum, Maggie, Stevie... Maggie's mum... Tony? All my friends are in London. And if I am very honest, many are more colleagues than friends. I'm not sure how long I'll be keeping in touch with the majority of them. Not a great indicator of a friendship, is it?

"Oh yes, you definitely should! And I'm glad I've bumped into you – I wanted to invite you. I can't believe we don't see each other more often, actually, living next door!"

"Oh, thank you, that's really kind." In comes my smooth, well-practised 'thank you but no thank you'... "I'm actually busy tonight, though." I have long since realised I don't have to justify myself with a reason not to do something I don't want to. In fact, the fewer details, the better – it makes it harder for anyone to suggest a way that you could rearrange your original plans. It does, however, mean I will need to stay out of the way tonight.

"Oh, that's no problem. The party's tomorrow!"

"That's great!" Damn. Can I get away with saying I'm busy tomorrow night, too? I could... yet I find myself saying, "Thank you, Stacey. That would be lovely."

"Fabulous! Come as you are, no need to make any special effort." Is it my imagination or is she eyeing my jeans and trainers? "Oh, and you know Maggie, don't you? If you see her, can you tell her she's welcome too, and her little girl? I've left a couple of messages for her, but she hasn't replied. Guess she's got a problem with her phone again."

"Yes, maybe." It would appear Maggie's trying her best to avoid this woman, too. She goes up even further in my estimation, for boldly ignoring Stacey's attempts at communication. I realise that sounds a bit cruel, but it doesn't sound like there is much love lost between the two of them and life is short. There's not time to waste on people we don't like.

In Marks & Spencer, I load up my basket with extra treats for me and Mum. I also ring her to ask if there's anything specific she needs, and if I can spend the evening with her.

"Of course you can!" She sounds so pleased, I feel guilty that the reason I'm asking her is because I now need to be out of the house to justify my earlier lie to Stacey. I could, of course, just say that my plans were cancelled – and that's assuming Stacey actually gives a monkey's what I do with my time. But I'm glad, really, to be able to cheer Mum up. She's had an extra lonely time, being stuck in her house these last couple of weeks.

I park at the Saltings, take my bags in, and unpack the food bags before I go into my bedroom and close my blinds to try on the jeans. I don't know why I bother closing the blinds – nobody overlooks this place, and I think the only way anyone could possibly see me would be in the unlikely event of them spying on me via binoculars from the cliffs on the other side of town – or passing by on the coast guard's helicopter. To go to such lengths just to watch me getting changed suggests more than a little desperation.

I turn on the light, easing off my designer trousers to pull on these loose, baggy garments. I do up the buttons and turn around to see how they fit me. I do like the way they look from behind. But they are so far from my usual get-up. When I pull the screwed-up paper out of my trainers and slide my feet into these soft, flat shoes, doing up the laces, I almost laugh. I look like I'm dressing up as Ada and her friends. Actually, no, I look like Maggie (albeit an older version). Still, I feel quite comfortable. And these are practical clothes. Unless it's raining, in which case surely these jeans will soak up all the puddles like litmus paper. I take a few steps in the trainers. I can almost feel my feet spreading already. I also look shorter than normal – even my most casual boots have a bit of a heel. I don't know about this. But together, these clothes have come to just over a hundred pounds. Normally, I'd spend that on one pair of jeans. I may as well hang on to them, and try them again another day.

Once I am dressed again, and feeling more like myself, I make a cup of tea and open one of the M&S pre-prepared salads, then sit down and switch on the TV. It feels slovenly, eating like this. I'll have to watch myself – first the jeans and trainers, next eating lunch on my lap in front of *Countdown*. It's a slippery slope.

Ada rings just as I am washing my cup and rinsing out the plastic salad-wrapping.

"Hi Mum! Are you OK? How was the food hub?"

"Oh, good, thanks. I feel like a bit of an outsider still, but I suppose it's been a while since I was a noob anywhere." I knew my use of the word 'noob' would make her laugh.

"Mum! Nobody says noob anymore."

"So you need to keep me informed about these things! Now, how's your week been?" She is in her first year of studies at Sussex University, doing Art History and Anthropology, and costing me a small fortune. For what, I have no idea – what can one do with Art History and Anthropology? Still, she had her heart set on it, and she's a hard worker. And a degree's a degree, I suppose.

"Oh... good, thank you. Lots to do, and lots of parties, too."

"Not too many, I hope?"

"Can there be too many parties?" I can just picture her grin. How I long to see it for real.

"Yes!" I laugh. "There can. But as long as you're being sensible..."

"Mum! I am always sensible."

"Good."

I don't need to go into details. And I mean sensible from a whole range of angles. Drink, drugs, sex. They may all be going on, I'm not stupid – I was young, and a student, myself once – but there is a right way and a wrong way to do these things. I hope that Ada is smart enough to do them the right way.

"I was just ringing to check in, really. I'm about to head out, with Rachel."

I can hear voices in the background – male and female.

"Not just Rachel, by the sound of it?"

"No, she's got some of the guys from her course here, too. You'd approve actually, we're going to a little arty cinema. And the film's in French!"

"You're right, I do approve. I hope they've got subtitles, though – French was never your strong point."

"Thanks very much! What are you doing this weekend?"

"Well, I'm going to see Mum tonight—"

"Is she feeling better?"

"She's getting there."

"Tell her I said to get well soon."

"I will... and then I'm going to a party tomorrow."

"Ooh!"

"But I don't want to."

"Whose party is it?"

"The neighbours' – the family I told you about."

"Well, you might surprise yourself and enjoy it. You could meet someone interesting!"

She has never given up on the idea that I might finally meet somebody long-term.

"You never know!" I laugh. "Now you go on, enjoy the film."

"I'll try. Love you."

"Love you too."

A phone call with my daughter never fails to make me smile.

2001

"Gosh, Louisa, you had us all worried there." Teresa's concerned face was the first thing Louisa saw. The men had all retreated to a safe distance, and were talking in awkward, hushed tones. For all the macho bravado of the office, the news about Gianni had hit everybody hard, on top of the shock and anxiety from watching the rolling news of the last few hours. Now the iron-clad Louisa Morgan had gone and collapsed. What was going on?

"What happened?"

"You passed out. Gerald... Mr Lacey... had just told us all about poor Mr Capaldi, and the next thing we knew, you were on the floor."

"Oh." Louisa felt sick. But she had to remain discreet. Even in her stupefied state, she knew that. For Gianni. "I guess it's all been a bit too much. I didn't sleep last night, watching it all. And I haven't really eaten this morning. Or last night," she admitted.

"No, I know, it's hard to feel like eating when the world's falling apart." Louisa had never really said more than a handful of words to Teresa before and now she looked at this woman in front of her, with tears in her eyes, like she was seeing her properly for the first time. She was suddenly ashamed of the way she had looked down on the women whose jobs seemed to be to prop up the men. Assistants, not ambitious enough to do a proper job. Behind every successful man is a woman. Was that the right saying? In reality, behind a lot of these successful men would be more than one woman. A mother, a wife, a personal assistant or secretary, or both. And these women actively encouraged it. Like they couldn't do the jobs themselves. That's how Louisa had thought. What a horrible snob she was. And she was so busy rivalling 'the boys' that she had never even considered her female colleagues, in more junior roles.

"You're exactly right. It does feel like the world is falling apart."

Teresa, in an instant of instinct and wholly natural feeling, put her arms around Louisa then and, after a split second, Louisa reciprocated. There was some comfort there.

"It's terrible," Teresa said. But she was already pulling herself straight and strengthening her jaw. "Unimaginable. But we need to carry on. You need to eat something. And I must arrange some flowers. And a card. Do you think we should sign it personally and send it, or shall I just get one printed and sent? It would get there quicker that way."

It took Louisa a moment to register what Teresa was asking. "Flowers?"

"Yes, we should, don't you think? It seems only right."

"For...?"

"Mrs Capaldi. Gianni's wife."

Louisa was grateful she was sitting down, and no doubt white as a sheet anyway. Nevertheless, she felt the room swaying. Teresa looked even more concerned.

"I'm making you a hot, sugary tea," she said. "And I'll send out for some pastries. You look like you could do with something sweet."

Teresa stood up and clicked off on her heels to the kitchen.

Louisa could not imagine wanting to eat anything, ever again, but when Teresa handed the steaming mug to her, she gratefully accepted it, if only to feel its warmth in her hands. Her head was pounding, and she could only manage a few sips before she felt like she would throw up. Even the smell of it made her feel sick. She thought she might never enjoy a cup of tea again.

Later, Teresa brought in a card, which had already been scrawled on by a few of their colleagues. The usual messages of sympathy, well-meant and sincere, but empty of anything of any real use.

Louisa stared at the card. At the blank spaces, waiting to be filled. This would eventually arrive in the hands of Mrs Capaldi. Gianni's widow. Who she had no idea had even existed. She should have known, of course. A man that age, of that status, so well presented and so at ease with the world and his place in it. *Behind every successful man is a woman.* More than one. A case in point. Gianni had a wife, and a mistress. The very word made Louisa's stomach turn and churn.

She picked up a pen and slowly pulled the lid off, and then she wrote.

I'm sorry. So very, very sorry.

She didn't sign her name, but slid the card back into the brown memo folder, and handed it back to Teresa with a thin smile. "Poor woman."

"I know. It's not like a card will help, or flowers. I know all that. But at least she will know we're thinking of her."

Louisa could barely think about anything else.

Louisa

I can hear the party before I leave my flat – banging bass from some club-type music that Ada would probably like, which suggests Sean or Stacey are trying too hard to be retain their youth. There is loud laughter, and the sound of corks popping, from the direction of their balcony (on the floor above, but I can hear it from my bedroom window). Their maisonette occupies part of the top floor, meaning it is half-penthouse. I did look at the smaller penthouse, but I didn't like the way the balcony was adjacent to the neighbours'. A lucky bit of forethought, as it turns out. I imagine sitting out there with Stacey on the neighbouring balcony, topping up her tan and letting out a stream of consciousness to which I am only required to nod and smile and signal agreement in all the right places.

But I am accepting their hospitality tonight, I remind myself. They didn't have to invite me. I need to learn to be more gracious, and less cynical. But I'm still jealous of Maggie, who has found a way to dodge the bullet.

"Hi Louisa!" She had greeted me warmly in the little local corner store. I was looking for a suitable bottle of wine to take – and a nicer one to crack open at home later. I know that sounds mean, but when you go to a party, you never know what's going to happen with drinks. Maybe I'd take an excellent bottle, only for it to be whisked away and put on a sideboard, while a glass of Lambrusco is thrust into my hand. Later on, I'd see some red-faced friend of Sean's clutching my nice bottle and sloshing it into the glass of the woman they're trying to pull – or slugging straight from the bottle. Of course, I have no idea who Stacey and Sean's guests are going to be. They may be well-mannered, sophisticated individuals who appreciate a good glass of red as much as I do. And yet, as I hear another pop of a cork and a resounding cheer, I fear not.

"Maggie!" I'd said, finding I was genuinely pleased to see her, "How are you?"

"Oh, good, thanks."

"Is your mum settling in OK?"

"Yes, she seems to be." Maggie's cheeks dimpled. "Thanks again for having Stevie last week. Actually, she's just over there, by the magazines... Stevie!"

At her name, the girl came round the corner, smiling as she saw me. "Hi, Louisa."

"Hello, Stevie. It's nice to see you. Are you picking out a magazine?"

"I'm looking, but they're too young, or too *girly*." She screwed up her face with evident displeasure. "Like, they've got make-up and stuff for their free gifts."

"What about a Lego one?" Maggie suggested. To me, she said, "They're so expensive, though."

"How much?"

"About five or six pounds a time."

I could see Stevie listening to this. "We don't have to get one, Mum."

"No, it's fine, I promised you."

"But there's not even one I really like. Can we get a book instead?"

"OK," her mum conceded. "But we won't be able to get one today. Maybe tomorrow, when we go to visit Granny. Tell you what, let's get a bar of chocolate for tonight."

"You're not going to Stacey's party?" The words were out of my mouth before I'd had time to think.

"Ah, no, unfortunately–" I wasn't convinced by this sentiment – "we don't have childcare tonight. Mum's out with her friend, and I didn't want to ask Elise, while she's still only just getting better."

"I could do it, and you could go in my place," I suggested, only half-joking. "Look, I've even picked out some wine for you to take!"

Maggie laughed. "I wondered if you'd be going. That would make it a bit more fun." I experienced a little inward glow that she thought I might be fun. "But no, that's fine."

"I thought you were old friends?"

"Yes, we have known each other a long time." A diplomatic response.

"Well, I'm sorry you won't be there. I don't suppose I'll stay long myself."

"I hope you have a good time," said Maggie.

"Yes. Thanks." Holding a bottle in each hand, I gestured towards the till. "I'd better get going. Have a good night yourselves. See you soon."

"Bye, Louisa," they chorused, endearingly similar in tone. They turned the corner to peruse the chocolate bars, and I went to pay for my wine.

There is clearly something underneath the surface

with Maggie and Stacey. Surely if your twin sister's best friend was throwing a party, you'd go to it, even if she wasn't your own best friend... unless there was a particular reason not to. It is none of my business, though, and I will just have to be envious of her for having a bona fide reason to give it a miss.

It takes a while for somebody to answer the door. I am debating whether to ring the bell again (and also wondering if I can get away with sneaking back to my flat instead), but just as I raise my hand—

"Louise!" It's Stacey, clutching a bottle of prosecco.

"Louisa," I corrected her.

"Stacey," she corrected me, kissing both my cheeks – or the air to either side of them. "But not to worry. Come on in and meet the gang!"

For the amount of noise coming from the flat, there are not all that many people in here. I recognise Sean, in an open-necked shirt and beige trousers, standing with a few other similarly dressed men. On the sofas are a few women, a bit more glamorous than their men, most around Stacey and Sean's age, but one looks more my kind of era – and she looks so like Stacey she can only be her mum.

Stacey picks a champagne flute from a tray stacked with them – they must be expecting a lot more guests – and pours some prosecco in, handing the glass to me. She selects a clean glass for herself as well, fills it, and clinks it against mine. "To good neighbours."

"To good neighbours."

"That's when good neighbours become good friends!" the older woman sing-songs and I am not so out of touch that I don't recognise the reference to the once incredibly popular Australian soap opera. I smile politely.

"Good one, Mum!" Stacey says. The woman stands up, and comes towards us, holding out her hand. Her nails are even longer than her daughter's. "I'm Sarah. Stacey's mum."

"Nice to meet you." I take her hand. "Louisa." I note Stacey's eyes flick to me, no doubt wondering why I keep calling everyone Louisa.

"So you've got one of these beautiful places too?"

"I have. I'm very lucky."

"I thought about getting the one above, but Stacey wouldn't hear of it."

I smile politely. "That's a shame."

"Yeah, I think she thinks it's too close for comfort." She nudges Stacey, who just smiles.

"I'm sure my daughter would be the same."

"Oh, how old's your daughter?"

"Nineteen."

"Really?" Sarah doesn't even try to hide her surprise. Her plucked-then-drawn-back-on-again eyebrows rise high above her thickly mascaraed eyes.

"Yes. I was an older mum," I say, inwardly kicking myself for this justification that I keep vowing not to make.

"Well, how old are you?" Sarah asks bluntly.

"Mum!" Stacey at least seems to have a little more idea of social nicety than her mum.

"You don't mind, do you?" Sarah peers at me.

"No, not really. I mean..." Is there really any point saying it's a bit rude? No, I decide. "I'm in my sixties." That should do.

"Oh, me too, believe it or not." I believe it. "And a grandmother!" I am sure she thinks this is too far beyond credence.

"Oh yes, I've seen Stacey's boys around. Are they here?"

"They're in the den," Stacey says, "on the X-Box. I tell you what, I'll take you to say hello, and give you a tour of the flat."

"Lovely."

The 'den', as Stacey calls it, is adjacent to the open-plan kitchen-diner. The boys, to their credit, all look away from the enormous screen to say hello to me, as instructed by their mother. They are dressed smartly, in the shirts and jeans I'd seen in Stacey's arms yesterday, all with their blond hair gelled stylishly, and young, eager faces flushed from the excitement of whatever game they're playing.

"Josh!" exclaims the youngest one. "You restarted without me!"

"You should have been looking, then."

"Josh," their mum says, fondly, with minimal warning in her voice.

"Nice to meet you," I say. "Enjoy your game."

"Thanks," they chorus.

"They'll be out for some food in a bit, I'm sure," Stacey says, leading me smoothly away from the den and up the stairs. The walls are adorned with photos of the boys, as babies, as toddlers, all evidently taken in a studio, with plain backgrounds and professional lighting.

Upstairs, there is a huge family bathroom, with 'jack and jill' doors leading off either side, into two of the boys' rooms – Jason's and Jamie's. It seems Stacey and Sean like alliteration. Josh as the eldest has the room next to his mum and dad's, also benefitting – as theirs does – from a balcony. The boys' rooms, which I feel guilty entering but which Stacey insists on, are all spotless and stylish, with TVs built into the ends of the beds, and expensive-looking bedding and framed pictures on the walls. I wouldn't say that Ada went without by any means, but this to me is a whole new level.

The pièce de resistance in this beautiful flat has to be the master bedroom. It is not much bigger than mine, and the view is very similar, but the en suite bathroom is something else. It has a step-up bath with colour-changing LED lighting, which Stacey has left on, and a huge window with a built-in blind that can be opened to look onto the bedroom and across to the balcony and the sea beyond. I can't decide if I like it or find it completely ridiculous.

We step out onto the balcony, and I peer down to one side, where I can see my own bedroom window. I'm glad my own little balcony is around the corner, and perhaps doesn't have quite the view this one does, but it is at least not overlooked.

To the right is the neighbouring balcony. The doors to it are closed. I have yet to meet whoever lives here. I say so to Stacey.

"Oh yeah, they've not moved in yet. I think it might be a holiday let." She rolls her eyes.

"Ah, it's not ideal," I agree, "but these places are expensive. I'm surprised, really, that two of them are actually residential. It's a bit of an issue for people locally. And although there's some affordable housing linked to this place, I can see it might feel like a bit of a kick in the teeth."

"It's just life, though, isn't it? I'm not going to feel guilty."

"No, well, I don't suppose I feel guilty exactly, either," I admit, loath to find some common ground between us.

"Someone's got to live here," she says glibly. And that does make me a bit uncomfortable. Because why should it be me? Why should it be Stacey? But then, I've worked hard. And I'm giving something back, aren't I? At the food hub. I could equally ask why it shouldn't be me.

When we go back downstairs, Sean is with his mother-in-law, who waves me over. Stacey goes in the opposite direction.

"Louise!" Sarah says.

"Louisa," Sean corrects her, and I give him a grateful smile. Sarah, however, seems not to notice.

"So how are you liking living here? From London, aren't you?" she asks.

"I've moved back from London," I say. "I was born here – lived right up there when I was a baby," I gesture to the cliffs on the outskirts of town, which are just visible from here.

"Oh really? I didn't realise that," says Sean.

"We're northerners, aren't we Sean?"

"I'd never have guessed," I say smoothly, and Sean suppresses a smile. I am warming to him.

"Aye, from Leeds originally," Sarah continues, "but Rob – my ex-husband – got a job down this way. We snapped up a bargain with our house, Cornwall weren't as popular as it is now."

"Lovely," I say.

"Anyway, we went our separate ways, and I moved

back up north with Stace, and she met you, didn't she, Sean? Then she decided she wanted to be back down here. When the boys came along. I've just come down for the week. I'm thinking of moving back though, too."

I glance at Sean, whose expression remains neutral.

"One of my old friends has come down this way," Sarah goes on. She clearly enjoys the sound of her own voice. "She's got a place in the next town along. One of her daughters is here though, one of Stacey's school friends."

"Oh, you mean Maggie?"

"That's her! Mousey Maggie." Sarah laughs.

"She's alright," Sean says, screwing up his face in annoyance. And it takes me a moment, but something clicks inside my mind. I realise who he reminds me of, but I can't compute it just yet. Not while Sarah's still blathering on.

"Oh, she's a nice girl, I grant you, but compared to Julia – that's her sister –" Sarah says, "Julia's a jewel, and Maggie's a mouse. That's what I always used to say."

"I know Maggie," I say, and offer nothing else.

"Do you really? It is a small world! Well, I suppose it's a small town, isn't it?"

"Yes, it is. She's been a wonderful friend and support to my mum, while I haven't been here. She and her daughter." I look from Sarah to Sean. His face has reverted to 'neutral'. I suspect he has had a lot of practice.

"It'll be good to see her again," Sarah says, and I think, *I'm not sure she'd say the same about you.* "And Lucy," she goes on, "the girls' mum, I mean. Me and her were friends and, well, we didn't fall out exactly, but it's all a long time ago, and water under the bridge…"

Sarah trails off, and it's the first time she's sounded

uncertain about something. This is all very intriguing. There are clearly a few unresolved issues. And I am not one to gossip, or to delve into other people's problems – god knows I've got enough of my own to worry about – but it's interesting. Let's leave it at that for now.

I stay at the party until just after ten, which I consider a reasonable time to leave. I plead tiredness, and I really don't mind if they consider me boring. But most of the guests are much younger than me, and I've exhausted my stock of polite conversation, and patience. These are some heavy, practised drinkers, it seems – and I know I like a drink, but I don't like to get 'out of my head' as Ada calls it. Or is it 'off my head'? Either way, I don't like it.

Stacey gives me a warm hug, and calls across to Sean, who smiles and waves. Since we established my connection to Maggie, he seems to have kept a bit of a distance. I am fairly certain that I know why.

2001

It was almost laughable, how despite everything – the hours she put in at work; the studied aloofness, cutting out any chance of close friendships; the ruthlessness she had created and mastered in order to further her career unhindered by her gender – Louisa had ended up pregnant, by a married man. Not just any married man, but the managing director of the company she worked for. Almost laughable, but not quite.

At first, she had been ill with the pregnancy, and it was hard to distinguish between the classic symptoms, which were not – despite what people might have you believe - confined to the mornings, although they were certainly worse then, and a general feeling of nausea at what had happened at the World Trade Center – and specifically to Gianni – mixed in with a low-level sickness at the situation she now found herself in.

And yet... as time progressed, a new and unexpected feeling crept in. Something like excitement. And sometimes almost contentment. As her belly filled and rounded, and she began to notice the fluttery movements inside her, it was as though her life was filling and rounding too. She resisted the feeling, it going so very much against what she had always believed and fought for, that a woman's life did not have to be fulfilled by motherhood, which inevitably meant having to put one's own needs and wants at the bottom of the pile. And yet...

She told Elise that she had planned it.

"I knew I wanted a baby," she said. "I never thought I would but then, I did. And so I made it happen."

Ada's grandmother (on the maternal side) had no idea who the father was, and Ada's grandmother on the paternal side had no idea who Ada was, or indeed who Louisa was. Louisa had no idea whether Gianni and his wife – she shuddered at the thought – had children, in which case Ada would have half-siblings, but she could think of no way to find out and, she told herself, it was not relevant anyway. They would be on different continents and very unlikely to ever meet.

She hired a doula to see her through the birth, and for a while it felt as though they were really friends. Bernadetta was much less of a hippy than Louisa had expected, and she seemed to be genuinely engaged with mother and daughter. And Louisa found she was bursting with such pride at this miracle of a baby, that she believed Ada almost certainly stood out from other babies, and Bernadetta could probably see that, too. But of course, new mothers-to-be came along one after another, and although Bernadetta really did care, it was no more or less than she cared about all her clients. And she answered Louisa's messages politely and softly, but gradually withdrew, knowing her boundaries. In time, Louisa would come to understand and appreciate that, and respect the professionalism with which Bernadetta worked, but at first it smarted.

Elise had offered to come and help, but something in Louisa had made her say no. She knew it was tied up with her feelings about her own childhood. And she also knew that was vastly unfair. Nevertheless, she determined she would conquer motherhood on her own terms. It was a wrench, going back to work, and entrusting Ada's care to Georgie, who turned out to be worth her weight in gold, but Louisa had to keep her job. She couldn't let everything she had worked for slip away. Yet all day long, Louisa would look forward to returning home, making every effort to be back in time to do her daughter's bath and bed, knowing that her male colleagues might still be in the office – or even at the pub – while their wives took care of their children. But Louisa would not have had it any other way, and the sight of her soft, shiny daughter wrapped in a coat of bubbles, giggling away in the bath or pushing a boat around making a *put-put* engine sound, filled her with unimaginable joy. Then, once Ada was softly sleeping, Louisa could drag out a stool at the kitchen counter – her preferred place to work – and switch on her laptop, then pop the cork on a bottle, and get back to work.

It did not always go according to plan. Ada might wake unexpectedly. She might have a sickness bug, or decide she just wasn't in the mood for going to bed. But Louisa would take a deep breath, knowing that at some point her daughter would surely go to sleep, and then she could get that work done. Even if it meant only being able to shut her eyes for a couple of hours before getting up and beginning everything all over again.

Bernadetta had moved on, and Georgie was too young to feel like a real friend. Plus, she was Louisa's employee, and Louisa knew full well that she had to maintain a professional relationship with her. Friends were a little on the light side, and friendships not too deep. And despite the joy she felt with Ada, there was a profound sadness in Louisa, which she was trying very hard to unpick. Clearly it was tied up with Gianni, who had let her down firstly by dying and secondly by being married – or maybe it was the other way around. And then there was his death –the very nature of it. The absolute knowledge that human beings are capable of doing the worst things to each other. And this wasn't new – Louisa was aware of that. Ever since humans had been around, they had been appalling to each other. Not all humans, of course. But great big gangs of humans, teaming up to fight against other gangs, or worse, persecute people who had no wish for violence or antagonism. All for the most ridiculous of reasons. If it wasn't religion, it was skin colour, or which football team someone supported, or just where somebody happened to live.

Perhaps with motherhood had come an awakening to the reality of these kinds of things. The rapes, the murders, the stabbings which happened in this city weekly, maybe daily. Not just because she was scared for her daughter's safety as she grew up, in a world where schools had lockdown policies, and metal-detectors to check pupils didn't have knives concealed on their persons. It wasn't just for Ada. It was for everyone. All the kids. All the adults. The people she passed on the streets in their sleeping bags, with their matted hair and dirt-ingrained skin. Because every one of these people had been a baby once. Every one of the people who committed these atrocious acts had been babies, too. As innocent and pure as Ada. What on earth had happened to them? And why them, not somebody else? There was no making sense of it.

She tried more than once to put this in words to John, her new therapist, who was kind and of course bearded, and had a beautiful, clean, calm study where they met once every one or two weeks. He smiled and listened and nodded, and every now and then would interject with something wise. And he told her that when his mother died, and his father not long after, he had begun to question everything. The point of everything. Reaching the conclusion that there was in fact no point. But also realising that there didn't have to be.

"What would you say, Louisa, if I were to ask you why you do what you do? Why you work so many hours? Why you're so driven to succeed?"

"I don't know. Why don't you ask me?"

He'd smiled, and the clock had ticked from the bookshelf, the sound reminding Louisa of Elise's sitting room back in Cornwall.

"Sorry, just being a smartarse," she'd said, when John had offered nothing more. He was good at these silences, which provoked thought, and further comment. "I'd say I do it for Ada."

"But you were doing it long before her, from what you've told me."

"Yes, you're right. I was. Now she's the driving force."

"And before?"

"Before... I don't know. I don't think I ever questioned it."

"And does it make you happy?"

"Happy? I'm not sure about that."

"Then why do you do it? After you've gone today, I'd like you to think about why we do things like pursue careers, relationships, friendships, if they don't make us happy."

Happiness wasn't really at the forefront of Louisa's mind. She wasn't sure she knew exactly what it was, although having Ada had at least given her a glimpse. It had stayed with her, that question, though, and when it came to applying for school places for Ada, she found herself choosing not private schools, where competition and educational success were heralded above all else, but more ordinary (although of course good) state schools, where her daughter would mix with lots of different people, and where Ada might find happiness in something that suited her, as she had in art, and English, and music. And her girl had done well at school – very well, in fact; Louisa couldn't help feeling proud of her daughter's excellent academic results – but she had also made strong, lasting friendships, and she had a social life, and was invited on a holiday with her friend's family. These surely were also markers of success, if happiness was the aim.

It seemed to Louisa that somewhere along the line, things had got confused. John was right – the whole point was happiness, wasn't it? And many, many people had lost sight of what happiness actually was.

And so Ada grew up in a far more relaxed way to what people would have imagined Louisa creating for her daughter. She could choose what made her happy, at school – just as long as she worked hard. She could have friends round whenever she liked, within reason – just as long as she worked hard. Because, while Louisa understood now that happiness was the key, she also knew the value of hard work, and the rewards it would bring in the long run. And she needed to know that her daughter, just like herself, and her mum, and her mum's mum before her, would know how to work. That way she would never be beholden to anyone.

Louisa

When I wake up early on Sunday with a clear head, I get straight out of bed. It won't be long before the mornings are dark well after 7am. Will it be lonely, waking up here, waiting for the daylight to catch up with me? It will take some acclimatising. Winter is not the best time for me. While I am not prone to depression exactly, I do find my spirits droop somewhat. I would normally just throw myself even harder into my work.

I step outside into a quiet world, which is warmer than it should be at this time of year, to my mind. The Cornish climate is often a degree or two above the rest of the country anyway, but I realise my scarf and gloves – which I took some pleasure in putting on – are not necessary. Not in town, at the very least. The harbour is calm and quiet right now, with a few gulls bobbing on its surface. I see a drinks can also, and a crisp packet, and they sadden me. I realise it may not be that somebody has deliberately thrown them into the water, but it's unnecessary, and it's a bad look.

I have no particular destination in mind, but I find myself heading up and out of town, towards the little row of cottages where I lived for the first few years of my life. The sky lightens as I go, and the deep, soulful sea mirrors it, welcoming the new day.

There is a wide pavement now, up the hill, but when we lived up here, and Mum had to get Laurie to school – and cart me about at the same time – it was nothing like this. She had no car; no choice but to walk. No wonder she's so bloody strong still. It's quite a steep incline, and I feel my face warming as I go. I unzip my coat.

My memories of this place are vague and uncertain, yet I find myself overcome with something as I near the top of the hill, where there once was a path – now a narrow driveway – to our little home.

Something about the word 'home' doesn't fit. I am largely relying on my brother's memory to come to this conclusion, but from what he's said, it wasn't a home – or not a happy one, at least.

"Dad was a bastard." Over the years, Laurie has expanded on this. Dad never hit him, but he was a bully – and Laurie thinks he came close, even though Laurie was just a handful of years old by the time Dad died. What kind of grown man hits a small child? His own small child, no less. My brother apparently did not match our dad's ideal of what a boy should be. Did our dad hit our mum? Laurie is sure that he did.

I'd felt angry at Mum, when I was growing up – that she'd let this man into her life, and she'd stayed with him. Made us stay with him. I had no idea.

Teenagers. They have to be selfish, I know. But seriously – my brother told me that our dad used to abuse our mum, and I had the audacity to be angry at her! I see it now. She was an orphan, in the post-war years. Her school had brought her here for safety, but she had got older, past school age, and the education system had churned her out – she was still down in Cornwall, with no home to go back to. What would have happened to Mum if it weren't for Angela Forbes? What would have happened if it weren't for Davey Plummer? But she was destined to marry. They all were – the alternative to face life as a spinster, as was the accepted term back then. The thought makes me shudder.

I walk quietly along the little driveway and look at the cottages. Ours was the one on the end. They are pretty little buildings – not a lot to them, all now extended at the rear, by the looks of it, and a couple with dormer windows, too. Making the most of the space and the views. Each now has its own little driveway, with just enough space for one car, and flowerbeds and hedgerows lining neat little squares of lawn. There is a trampoline in the garden that belongs to our old house – and a neat raised bed, with squashes and pumpkins creeping over the sides. Mum would be pleased about this. She talks about getting her taste for gardening while we lived up here. It's good to think she had some pleasure in her life back then. There is a large swathe of grass on the other side of the driveway, and a line of trees – bent double from the sea wind – forming a barrier between the neat little cul-de-sac and the sea. Around the feet of the trees are tangles of shrubs and brambles, where tiny birds go about their business. I am drawn towards the trees.

Where was it? Which is the exact spot where my dad died? Or where he had slipped – he more probably met his death on the rocks below, or on his way down – as a result of returning home drunk, as Laurie tells me was usual. Poetic justice. Davey Plummer had allowed his drinking to damage us all, but in the end it was his downfall. I trace the line of trees, hoping that none of the cottages' occupants are watching me, wondering what I'm doing. There is a fence here now as well, I notice, firmly rooted above the top of the slope. Very sensible. At a little gap between the growth, I peer over the top of the fence, and down the shockingly steep siding. I can't see the sea, but I can hear it – calm today, and soothing. Just pushing itself affectionately against the rocks, like a dog gently butting its head against its favourite human.

What was it like, the night that he died? Mum has told me so little, and I have never felt able to ask her. Maudie told me a little more. That it was a rainy night, and he must have slipped. Maybe he'd stopped to take a piss against the trees – although he was so nearly home, that doesn't make sense. What if he'd been so drunk, he'd had to stop and be sick, and had leaned on a tree for support, only to find it wasn't as firmly rooted as he'd expected, or he'd misjudged where he was leaning?

It's very strange, thinking of my own father in this way. Detached. It's like he wasn't real – like none of this was. I stop, take a few breaths, and think of John's advice to try and be 'present'. I am doing my best, but I want to touch the past. To know exactly what happened, and to find my father, somehow. I don't have to love him – I don't think I could – but I have carried his absence with me all my life. My father a constant, shadowy figure on the periphery of my vision. No matter which way I turn, or how quickly – or slowly – he remains out of reach. It is not lost on me that I have wilfully kept from Ada any knowledge of her father, but I thought at the time it could only do harm. Perhaps I was wrong. Maybe it is better to know the truth.

Further along the clifftop, just higher than the treetops, a kestrel hovers, wings occasionally beating to keep it in place, tiny legs tucked neatly beneath it, head fixed absolutely still, eyes intent on its prey. It stays like that for some time, and I watch it, until – instead of going in for the kill – it moves along, flying off and out of sight. I feel disappointed, although some small, furry creature has lived to see another day.

I don't know what I had expected to feel, coming up here. I have never known how to feel about my dad. I wanted to miss him, when I was growing up, and all my friends had their fathers. Children and adolescents can find all kinds of reasons to feel hard done by, and sometimes almost seem to relish in it. Even sunny, smiley Ada was like that, at times. I suppose I did miss him, in a way; if not as a person then a notional figure in my life. Laurie did his best to fill the gap, but he had his own problems. Mum did her best, full stop.

I stand here, somewhere close to the spot where my father died, and decide I am going to ask my mother about him. Today. This morning. I give myself no time to change my mind, and turn on my heel, heading back towards town.

I pick up some pastries at the bakery, and a bag of coffee from the corner store. A bottle of milk, too, in case Mum's running low. And, as an afterthought, some flowers. I am going to do better by my mum, and I am going to start now.

"Louisa!" she says, as usual pleased to see me. I remember how Ada's little face used to beam when I would go in to see her in the morning, or following her afternoon nap. Such unadulterated joy, whether I deserved it or not.

"Hi, Mum. I've brought us breakfast."

"Oh, that is lovely of you! I was just thinking I'm getting my appetite back."

"Well, that's good news. I've got pastries, and I've got coffee, if you'd like some? I'll make it."

"And the flowers?"

"For you, too. Of course. But not to eat," I say cheerfully, and Mum laughs.

She is beaming as I follow her through to the lounge, and we go into the kitchen. I put the kettle on, and Mum roots around for her cafetière while I get some plates from the cupboard.

"Is it cold out?" she asks.

"No, not really. Not at all, in fact. It feels like it might never get cold!"

"We'll have to wait till January for that," she says, and her words provoke a cough. She clearly isn't one hundred per cent recovered yet.

I run the tap and fill a glass of water for her.

"Thank you, love."

"You go and sit down, Mum. I'll bring these through, and some coffee in a minute."

"Oh, thank you. You are good."

"Not at all. And certainly not as good as I should be."

"Don't be so hard on yourself, Lou. You don't see how good you are."

Mum goes through to sit down. I am resisting using the word 'shuffles', as it conjures up an image of a slipper-footed, dressing-gowned geriatric – the last thing Mum would want to be – but she does look frail. In her thin cardigan, her shoulder blades look like they could slice through it. I put a smile on my face and bring the plate of pastries in, with two smaller plates. I place them on the dining table, as Mum has taken one of the hardbacked chairs there.

"Don't you want to be more comfortable? We could sit on the settee," I say.

"Oh no, I'm not giving in to that, thank you very much. We are having breakfast, we will sit at the breakfast table. And lunch table. And dinner..." she laughs, but it makes her cough again.

"Should you go to the doctors?" I ask.

"No, I'm feeling so much better, honestly. These things always leave me with a cough."

"If it gets worse, you should go and see someone."

"I will. I promise."

I go back into the little kitchen, and finish making the coffee, warming a small jug of milk in the microwave. "Don't wait for me, Mum, tuck in!" Of course, she waits for me to get back.

"This is lovely, Lou," she says, when I return with the coffee. "It really is so good having you close by."

"I really like it, Mum. I'm just sorry it's taken me so long to come back."

"Don't be silly!" Mum takes a gratifyingly big bite of pastry, tiny flakes adorning her lips and puffing in the air as she speaks. "You've done exactly the right thing with your life."

"I wouldn't have been able to do it without you though, Mum. You brought me and Laurie up, to have our own interests. You can see that from how bloody different we are!"

Mum laughs. "Well, I can't tell you what to like, can I? I'm your mum – your guardian – not your boss."

"I don't think I've ever really said thank you for it, though, Mum. But I am grateful."

"Oh shush," she says, "don't waste another moment thinking about it. You've done the same for Ada. It's how it works. It's what mums do."

"And dads?" I say.

"Some of them."

She is cool, my mum. A difficult woman to ruffle. Not that I am trying to ruffle her. But I am trying to find a way into this conversation.

"Did you miss him, ever?" I ask now.

"Who? Your father?"

"Yes."

"Louisa, if I am truly honest, then no, I didn't. In another world, another time, we might not have stayed together at all. It was different then, and so much harder to extricate yourself from a – what would Ada say? – a toxic relationship."

"Is that what it was?" I ask quietly.

"Well... yes. He was a troubled man. And a drinker."

"Were you scared of him?"

"Sometimes."

"I'm sorry, Mum."

"You have nothing to be sorry for. There will always be people better off than yourself, and there will always be people worse off. And it worked out in the end, didn't it? I had you and Laurie. And Maudie and Fred, and Angela. And then I had this house. I was very lucky. If I feel sorry for anyone, it's him."

"Who, Dad?"

"Yes. He wasn't a good husband, to put it mildly. But he had a tough childhood. His own father was not a particularly nice man. It's a pattern, isn't it? And here I am, past ninety – and there he was, cut off in his twenties. I sometimes think I can barely remember him, it was so long ago. I've lived so many decades since."

I am quiet for a moment. Stunned by my mum's capacity for forgiveness, and her balanced outlook.

"You are a wise woman, Mum."

She laughs, and I'm glad this time it doesn't result in a coughing fit. "I'm old, it's part of my job description!" She looks at the clock on the wall. "Oh goodness, is that the time?"

"Do you have somewhere to be?" I am suddenly wrongfooted. There was more I had wanted to discuss.

"Yes, I'm going to the Eden Project!"

"The Eden Project?"

"Didn't I tell you? Maggie's invited me, she's going with Stevie, and her mum."

"Oh."

"Look, why don't you come as well? If you've nothing else to do. I'm sure they'd be very glad to have you along. And I know I would."

Mum – my kind, thoughtful Mum – puts her hand on my arm and smiles into my eyes. I am disappointed that I don't have her to myself. That my imagined session of honesty and revelations is being cut short. But I look at my mother's face smiling at me and I think I would do anything for her. How could I say no?

This time, I insist on driving. It's expensive, paying for fuel, and I don't know what Maggie earns, but she's a single mum, working for a non-profit, and I don't imagine she's got a lot of excess cash. I don't say this, of course.

"Please let me," I say instead. "It's my heated seats – they're good for my back. It's been playing up lately."

"You didn't mention anything about your back." Mum looks concerned.

"Oh no, well, it does this from time to time. But I find using the heated seats in the car helps."

"And I don't suppose being squashed up in my little banger would be very helpful!" Maggie laughs, but there's no bitterness or sarcasm there.

When Lucy arrives, she, Maggie and Stevie sit in the back. Mum is up front with me. "I see what you mean about these heated seats!" she says. "Though it made me feel a bit like I'd wet myself at first."

"Mum!" I say, smiling at the guffawing from the back seat. Stevie in particular is delighted by this.

"Good job I've got my Tena Lady," Mum concludes, and Lucy has to explain to Stevie what that is.

"What, so when I'm old, I might have to wear nappies?"

"Never mind when you're old – when you're my age, if you've had kids, and you don't do pelvic floor exercises," says Maggie.

"Pelvic what…?"

"You'll find out in good time!" I say, moving the conversation briskly on. It feels quite potent, this car full of females, of all different ages. I wish Ada was here too – although I have no idea where we'd put her. In the boot, I suppose.

We arrive at the Eden Project and are ferried down the winding hillside on what they call the land train. I can't believe I haven't been here before. It's an incredible place, so beautifully tended that even at this time of year, when most of the flowers are long wilted and gone, it is colourful and mesmerising, with trees and leaves of so many different colours and shapes and textures – tall, fluffy grasses, and short, squat, fat bushes and shrubs. And the birdsong is spectacular.

Of the two biomes, we opt for the Mediterranean one first, with its warm, pleasant climate. It's a real treat at this time of year, as the heat of the summer is slowly leaking away, like air from a punctured paddling pool. Mum looks as relaxed as I have seen her in some time, and has a little colour in her cheeks.

"This suits you!" I say to her. She is leaning against a short wall. She may look well, but she is clearly still tired.

"It does. I love it. Maybe I should book a holiday, while I'm still well enough to travel." She is only joking, but I have a flash of inspiration for her Christmas present. A few days away, somewhere warm, in January or February. It would do us both good. Maybe Ada can come too, if I time it right.

Mum opts to stay put while the rest of us go into the hotter, rainforest-style biome. I buy her a cup of tea from the little café, then the four of us traipse across to the hottest place I have been in a long, long time. I do like it. I love the plants, and the birds, but the higher we get, the hotter it becomes, and it is a little stifling.

"It's a good job Mum didn't come to this bit," I say to Lucy.

"Absolutely. To be honest, I'm finding it a bit much myself."

"Let's go up there!" says Stevie, pointing to a precarious-looking, very high, walkway.

"Erm…" I say, at the same time that Lucy says a resounding "No!" and Maggie says, "Yes, let's do it!"

Lucy and I look at each other and laugh.

"We'll stay down here, and wait for you," says Lucy.

"Boring!" says Maggie. She is grinning from ear to ear, clearly revelling in the company of her mum and her daughter. She and Stevie rush off towards the climb, and Lucy and I find a spot near the waterfall, where it is a little cooler, although the noise makes it harder to hold a conversation.

"So are you settling in?" I ask her.

"Yes! Very much so. It was time for a change."

"It must be strange, leaving your family home."

"Well, yes, in a way. We had some good times there. Some great times. But it's only been me for so long now, and the garden was starting to become more of a chore than a pleasure, if you know what I mean."

"Yes, well, in a way. I did love my garden in London. But it was small and easy to manage. And I had a gardener," I say apologetically. "Completely frivolous of me, I could easily have looked after it myself, but I always had work to do. I did love my little outside space."

"Do you miss the city?"

"I suppose I do, in some ways. But not in others."

"I was born and brought up in Bristol," Lucy tells me. "Not as big as London, of course, but there was always something going on. I missed it, when we moved here. Sometimes I still do."

"It would be nice to have the best of both worlds."

"What, like a place out here, and a little flat in the city?"

"And a private jet to take us between them!"

"Oh yes, I can just see that."

She's a very easy person to be with, and it is just possible that she and I might become friends – if she would be open to it, of course. But it's a bit strange that the friendship which has brought us all together is between her daughter and my mum.

I find myself saying, "I met somebody who knows you, the other day."

"Oh yes? Is it Stacey?" Lucy asks, and I can sense rather than see a rolling of her eyes.

"Of course, there is Stacey, but I met her mother, too. At the housewarming party." I wonder if Maggie had actually even mentioned this party to her mum, but Lucy does not commit either way.

"Sarah?" she says, with a slight tone of distaste.

"Yes. She said she'd known you quite well in the past." I'm annoyed at myself for pursuing this line of conversation, which is clearly uncomfortable for Lucy, but now I don't know how to end it.

"Our husbands worked together."

"Oh, I see. I thought it was just that the girls were friends."

"No – well, they were. We were all new to the area at the same time, and the girls formed a bit of a trio, but you know what it's like when there are three–" I don't, but I nod my head as though I do – "and Stacey was a bit of a pain at times, to be honest. A bit competitive. When she realised she couldn't beat Julia, she took it out on Maggie. I mean, nothing major; just silly, childish stuff, really. But it used to annoy me. You can't tell them who to be friends with though, can you? No more than you can tell them who they should have a relationship with, when they're older, I mean."

"No, I suppose not. I'm a little ashamed to say, I don't know about my daughter's life in such detail. I know her friend Clara, and I know they have a wider group of friends – boys and girls. And now Ada's gone to university, but I haven't been to visit her."

"Oh, you should! Maggie went to Bristol, and I had some wonderful times staying with her, revisiting all my old haunts."

I find myself envying this easy way that Lucy seems to have weaving in and out of her daughters' lives.

"Is that where she met Stevie's dad?" I ask, and again I want to throttle myself. Why am I like this?

"Yes, I think so. He didn't stick around, to be honest. And I wasn't all that interested in him – just in her, and Stevie. It wasn't all that long since my husband died, you see. I think I just wanted my little family unit, or what was left of it. Julia was already with Paul, who she's married to now, and she had moved on. When Maggie came back, and Stevie came along, I had them all to myself. I wonder if I shouldn't have encouraged her more, to try and reignite whatever relationship she'd had, but I was selfish, and didn't want a stranger encroaching on our little world."

She is so open, and guileless. I am ashamed of my prying. "Do you know what? Fathers are over-rated. Or they can be," I correct myself. "I'm sure your husband was lovely."

"He was. Not perfect, by any means, but a good man."

"But I raised Ada by myself. Mum was on her own with me and my brother after our dad died. She was fantastic. Maybe Stevie's father would have very little to add – Maggie's clearly doing a wonderful job. Perhaps his involvement would have only made them all miserable."

Lucy smiles. "That's exactly what I think. But I don't like to sound like I'm anti-men. Julia's Paul, for example, is a fantastic husband and son-in-law, and a great friend to Maggie, too. And Jeff may have had his faults, but he loved his daughters, that's for sure. And now there's Tony…" Am I imagining it, or do I see a little hint of intrigue in Lucy's eyes now? Maybe I'm not the only one straying into subjects that I'm not sure I should. "You used to work with him, I think?"

"Yes," I say, "we worked quite closely together. He's another of the good ones."

"That's good to hear." She smiles, perhaps satisfied that there is nothing going on that she should know about.

"Granny!" I hear Stevie before I see her. She is streaming down the pathway, her cheeks flushed, and a beaming smile across her face. "That was amazing!"

Maggie is not far behind. She doesn't look quite so radiant. "Urgh. That was too high. And too hot. I thought I was going to throw up."

"But you didn't, Mum!" Stevie smiles at her proudly.

"No. I didn't. Now, we'd better go and find Elise," she says.

I had wanted to be the one to say that. But what does it matter, really?

When we return home, we are all in high spirits, and Mum suggests we get a takeaway from the chip shop.

"Shall we have them at my place?" I suggest. I don't want to sound like I'm bragging, but there's more space for five there.

"Oh no, that's fine, why don't you come to mine?" Maggie asks hurriedly. She clearly doesn't want to come to my flat, and I think I know why, but nobody else seems to notice. "It's closer to the fish shop, and Mum's car's there anyway, plus it's not so far for Elise to walk," she concludes, perhaps trying to convince herself as much as anyone.

"That's a good idea, Maggie," Mum says, and I feel slightly wrong-footed, as though she doesn't want to come to my flat. *Grow up, Louisa.* I park in a side street, and the five of us walk through the heavy near-dark of the late afternoon. It does feel something like cold now, although maybe that is just in contrast to the biomes we've been in today.

"Why don't Maggie and I go to get the food, and you three go in?" I suggest, as we reach Maggie's front door. "If we're quick, we'll be the first ones in the shop!"

This is the first time that it's been just Maggie and me. I notice she is quieter now, and perhaps less at ease. I remember Mum saying that Maggie is a worrier, and it annoyed me at the time, probably out of jealousy, but I feel for her now. Still, I can't quite help myself.

"I met Stacey's mum the other day."

"Oh god, did you?" She's not so nervous as to hold back her feelings on this subject.

"Yes!" I smile. "She's a bit of a character."

"That's one way of putting it."

"Maybe explains a bit about Stacey...?" I suggest.

"Yes, maybe, but I think we all take responsibility for ourselves. We can't blame our parents forever."

That is an interesting thing to say.

"Well, Ada can only have me to blame!" I say. "She's

never met her dad."

"Yes, Stevie's the same..." Maggie stops, as if she's thinking about what she's saying.

"Has she never met her dad, either?" I ask, playing the innocent.

"No," Maggie says firmly. "She hasn't."

But her reaction has confirmed my suspicions to me. Stevie almost certainly has met her dad; she just doesn't know it. From my conversation with Lucy, I have concluded that she genuinely has no idea as to his identity – or she is a very good actor. To my mind, the question is whether it can really be possible to keep something like this quiet? Every time I see those boys, and Sean, I more clearly recognise their resemblance to Stevie. Does Stacey not see it? Does Mum?

This is not the only thing I want to know from Maggie, though. As we approach the chip shop, I see it has not opened yet, so there is more of a chance to talk. But how do I phrase this one?

"How's Tony?" I opt for simple.

"Oh, he's good, thanks. Very good." She looks at me, like she has questions of her own. Which is good, because it must mean he hasn't told her anything. "Maybe we should all go for a drink sometime?"

I want to smile. She is sounding me out now, but I'm better at this kind of thing than she is. Clearly, she knows there is something there, some kind of history, but it would appear she has no idea what. Has she asked Tony? Is she scared to? I would tell her. I am not ashamed, and it would be good to tell her she has nothing to fear. That actually she and I have an awful lot in common, but it's not in the way that she suspects.

First, though, I need to tell my mum. That thing she said, when she was ill – about knowing about AJ – has kept popping back into my mind, niggling at me. I know what she thinks she knows, but she is wrong. I will walk back home with her after we've eaten, go in for a cup of tea, and I'll tell her about everything that has happened, including my relationship with Gianni. I desperately want life to be simpler, which means being more open. The sooner I begin, the better.

2020

Louisa loved the feeling of starting a whole new project, especially at the tail end of a year. It meant she had something to look forward to through the coldness of winter and it seemed especially uplifting after this year of covid. She was hopeful that the next year would bring change, for the better, but was grateful that she had something new and interesting to focus on should the worst happen and the country go into lockdown yet again. She imagined this feeling might be how it was for a writer, opening up a fresh new notebook (or a new Word document). The blankness, the possibility, like new-fallen snow, before there had been a chance for anything to tarnish it.

Her job would be to achieve a full understanding of what the client needed to achieve, draft out a plan, then pull together a team, comprised of clients and colleagues (ideally handpicked by her), then make this team mesh together, and do whatever it took to make the project succeed.

This project was personal. Based in the very town she had been born and brought up in, she already knew that the Saltings development wasn't popular amongst the locals, but that wasn't her problem. All permissions had already been sought and granted. The development had been approved long before, and the building work already nearly done. Canyon Holdings were now looking to her company, with its UK offices, to help see the project through to fruition.

A team of three was being sent from the States, who would be responsible overall, and it was up to Louisa to find the right people from her company to work with them and manage the supposedly softer side of the project; making it gel with the local economy, and local community. This would include a strong focus on communication, the PR – the smaller, nicer details, of which there were very many – to try and help this great big brash development ease its way smoothly into the small, down-to-earth fishing town. It was not going to be easy, but Louisa relished a challenge.

"Hi. I'm AJ." He thrust his hand towards her, his flawless teeth showing with his bright smile. She offered a subconsciously closed-mouth smile back. Maybe this was why Americans thought Brits were so inhibited. Perhaps it was just a case of trying to hide crooked, off-white teeth.

"Louisa Morgan. Pleased to meet you."

"I've heard great things about you, Louisa. I'm looking forward to working together."

A man and a woman walked into the room, also offering smiles and handshakes.

"This is Samantha Bernstein, and Tony Jones. From the New York office. Though Tony's one of you guys."

"Pleased to meet you, Louisa," said Tony, with a comfortingly familiar south-east accent. He was perhaps the same age as AJ – they were both younger than Louisa, but maybe not by too much. Tony had a friendly, open face, and a smattering of stubble. He also, Louisa noted, had clearly not been to the same dentist as AJ. His teeth were reassuringly uneven.

"I've heard so much about you!" Samantha gushed, taking Louisa's hand in both of hers. It was hard to gauge her age, but Louisa thought she must have at least a decade or two on this woman, who was slender and well-groomed, and immaculately made up – stopping just short of over-the-top. Her eyes were adorned with thick, dark lashes, and ringed with liner, while her lips were a soft, rosy red. Louisa normally didn't like lipstick, but on Samantha it looked good. Louisa had a feeling anything would look good on her.

"I'll get us some drinks," Louisa said. "Coffee all round?"

"I could drink a gallon," Samantha said. "I'm so jetlagged. I must look awful."

"Oh yeah, you're totally haggard," Tony grinned, and Louisa's antennae pricked up. Was this a workplace flirtation? It didn't matter to her. They were her clients, it was not her problem. Just as long as it didn't get in the way of the project.

"So you're really from Cornwall?" AJ asked Louisa in the restaurant that night. "What's it like?"

"Oh, it's... actually, it's beautiful. Stunning. People often can't believe I've left there. But it's also quiet, remote, detached, and there is a lot of poverty. Not much opportunity. I felt disconnected from the rest of the world when I was there."

"Not always a bad thing, right?" AJ asked softly. "I wouldn't mind feeling disconnected sometimes."

His words disarmed her. "I suppose New York is another step up – or twenty – from London. It's quite a full-on place to live and work, isn't it?"

"It is. And I do love it. I'm a proud New Yorker, born and bred."

"I could tell." She already knew his accent, its effects

tinged with a touch of longing. She had never quite forgotten Gianni. Well, she couldn't very well forget him, could she? Not with Ada a lifelong reminder. But even if it hadn't been for her daughter, Louisa knew that it would be a long time before she forgot Gianni. The intensity – and then the dreadful falling apart of everything, their relationship really the least of it all, measured against the events of 9/11. She had been duped by him and she had been angry about that, but she was also in an agony of hidden grief. There was too much to protect – starting with Gianni's wife, and ending with Louisa's career and reputation. It was why she had turned to John; seeing a counsellor was something she had never thought she would do, but it seemed a fittingly American solution to her problem.

"Have you been to the States?" AJ asked.

"A couple of times. I love it. But it's exhausting."

"It is. Sometimes I love it, too. Sometimes I hate it. I'm excited to be in London for a while."

"I hope you enjoy it. If there's anything you need while you're here, just ask."

"I'll be sure to." His dark brown eyes looked smilingly at her. Was he flirting? She couldn't tell. She shouldn't care. But she felt her body tense a little uncomfortably. She let her well-practised, straight-faced professional cover slide over her, and moved the moment on. "Will you be visiting Cornwall soon?"

"Not immediately, no. I'll be sending Sammie and Tony on ahead, as scouts. Not that I don't want to get out there. I can't wait to see it. Maybe you can show me around, tell me a bit about your wild teenage years."

"I'd be more than happy to." *Maintain the*

professionalism, Louisa. "I don't know about wild, though. The wildest thing about Cornwall is the weather." She inwardly groaned at this awful line. Still, better to appear dull and pour cold water on this potential flirtation, which she may have been imagining anyway.

Yet as time went on, and particularly during the weeks when Samantha and Tony were away, she knew she was not imagining it. AJ was refreshingly open with her, and had no problem sharing about his personal life. He was single, but had been married – no children. His mother had died relatively recently and he was impressed to hear about Elise, who was getting close to ninety but showing no signs of stopping, anything. His father had been regularly absent with work, but AJ had been close to him. He had died when AJ was in his early thirties, and it had pushed him to re-evaluate his life.

He'd been a bit of a party animal by the sound of it, but decided then and there to try and follow in father's footsteps – to be a great businessman, and a great father. He had always worked for his father's firm, but he left it to forge his own career. And he found a steady girlfriend, then asked her to marry him, although the marriage only lasted a handful of years, and his quest to become a great father as well as a successful businessman had not come to fruition. "Yet," said AJ, and Louisa felt a *flump* of disappointment within her gut. That was certainly not something she would be able to help him with. But he was already in his early fifties, and as was often the case, she felt the unfairness of it all. What woman of his age could possibly think of becoming a parent? She remembered how, as a pregnant forty-something she had been referred to as a geriatric mother. Geriatric, for god's sake! But none of that was AJ's fault. And she had to acknowledge that she liked the way he talked to her so openly.

She began to look forward to seeing him every day, and she missed him if he was not in the office.

While the others were down in Cornwall ("Trying to win hearts and minds," as AJ put it – Louisa knew that if anything, a confident American woman like Samantha would be more likely to lose hearts and minds in the 'quaint' little Cornish town, but she said nothing), AJ and Louisa worked long into the night together, sometimes just the two of them, and usually in Louisa's personal office – she had climbed out of the open-plan area some years ago now, and never looked back – which had an impressive view across Canary Wharf, of which AJ never seemed to tire.

She was careful to leave the door open at all times, and to maintain a respectable physical space between herself and her client, but AJ, while not pushy, seemed increasingly keen to get close.

"Shall we get something to eat?" he asked one night.

"Sure," she said. "There are some good places around here. A bit commercial, but good quality."

"I was thinking of somewhere a bit more intimate, maybe." His eyes sought hers.

The 'maybe' softened what might otherwise have been a strict, no-nonsense response from her. Memories of Bocca Felice threatened to flood her mind. She had not been there since Gianni.

"I don't know anywhere like that around here," she said. "Shall we just go to one of the pubs by the water?"

"Sure. Whatever you like."

She couldn't help but notice that he looked a little disappointed. But she couldn't do anything else. Never again was she going to let her guard down. And yet...

They ate, and they drank, and they talked. And they laughed. In a way that she hadn't laughed for a long time.

When AJ suggested he walk her home, she didn't say no. Nor did she resist when he kissed her, under a lamppost, amid a late-night mist.

"I feel like I'm in a film," he smiled.

"I know what you mean."

He didn't come in – not that night, at least. For one thing, Ada was at home, and Louisa never, ever brought men into the house with her daughter there. Ada knew that her mother dated, but she had never met any of Louisa's dates, because none of them had lasted long enough for Louisa to deem them worthy of meeting her daughter. More importantly, Louisa did not want to bring a strange man into their home, where Ada was prone to wandering around in nothing much more than a long t-shirt, or even sometimes just her underwear. Louisa wanted her daughter to always feel as comfortable in her own space as she did right now.

She kissed AJ again at her front gate, already transforming from lover to mother as she wondered whether Ada might be looking out of an upstairs window, but she need not have worried. The house was in darkness, Ada long since asleep. And despite the return to reality, the magic of the evening remained, floating around her as she walked up the path to her front door, and sneaking into the house with her like a little of the London mist.

Louisa

The first food hub meeting I attend is a lively affair. There are about fifteen of us, crammed into the space that also doubles as Tamsin's office. Tamsin works practically full-time here, but for a part-time wage. This is one of the matters up for discussion – fundraising to make hers a full-time paid position.

Jude is dressed a little more smartly than usual, and has made up her eyes today. It suits her. Makes her blue eyes more piercing than ever.

"You're certainly needed," Jude says, "and you will be all the more, if we get the Warming Ways and Baby Bank fully functional." She proposes that we set up a few local fundraisers, and apply for as many local sources of funding as possible. I can see that each one of these will take time, though, and may only produce a small amount of income. To me, the idea of local people fundraising for the hub also seems a bit counter-productive, and does not project a professional image.

I say so, adding, "I have an idea which might be a little easier."

Jude does not seem entirely welcoming of my input. I understand. I can be a bit supercilious. But I'm working on being less so.

"Go on," Jude says, magnanimously.

"Well, as I think you are all aware now, I have done quite a lot of work with the Canyon Holdings corporation. And I come from that world myself. So I know what kind of things they have to do, to appear morally upstanding—" there is an ill-concealed splutter from Matthew – "and also that they will have a budget for this kind of thing. A budget which will increase year on year. If we approach them now, I think there's a good chance that they might see this as an easy win."

"But we're five months away from the new financial year," Jude says. "That's a long time to wait."

"But all of the other sources you've mentioned will take a while to come to fruition. And think of the time involved with applying for or coordinating each one of them. My way will be a lot quicker and simpler."

There is an awkward silence as the others try to gauge Jude's reaction, and I wonder if I have overstepped the mark. I may sound like I'm being arrogant, but I actually have the best interests of the hub at heart. And there's no point beating around the bush. But I do also find that I have a desire to please Jude. I don't want to annoy her; I want us to be together on this.

"Alright," she says. "See what you can find out if you could, please. You are right, Louisa. We need the maximum resources possible concentrated on our operations here."

"Great." Now I am going to have to go cap-in-hand to Tony with this. At the same time, I've seen just how much these new ideas will help the local community – and also just how hard Tamsin works. My plan is to request more than has been proposed. I've been doing some digging around, looking at old job adverts, job descriptions, etc, and I have seen that Tamsin's wage is not much, even as a full-time position – nor is Jude's, for that matter, particularly given the level of responsibility she has. When I compare their salaries to those back in London, it all feels very wrong. My hope is that I can secure better pay for them both. It will also mean talking to the board of trustees, but that doesn't bother me. In fact, it's the part I feel most comfortable with. However, I don't want to tell Jude about any of this, in case I fall flat on my face. It will be an interesting test of whether I can wield any authority or influence these days.

The rest of the meeting is given over to the Christmas present-drive, which involves asking for donations of toys and adults' gifts, and finding a way to do this without alerting children and potentially ruining the magic of Christmas. Mark and Matthew go to different churches and say there is already something similar going on at each of them. Belinda's children attend the local primary school, and next week they are having a non-uniform day for a 'secret Santa' event closer to Christmas. It seems like all the local options are covered, and we draw a blank.

"Unless you can get your London mates to help with this as well?" Jude asks, and I can't tell if she is serious, or joking, or sneering at me.

"Actually, there is a scheme at my old place, for something similar. People bring in any empty shoeboxes they have, and everyone donates a gift or two, and there are some lovely ladies who spend their lunch hours packing them, and wrapping them."

"Always the ladies, isn't it?" Jude says.

"Sadly, yes." I meet her eyes and we find we agree on this at least. I don't want to add that I never got involved with it. I considered myself too busy and important. I was as bad as the men in that way.

"And where do the boxes go from there?" Jude raises her eyebrows.

"I... don't know," I concede. "But I can ask."

"You may as well," Jude says. "Tag it on to your other request." She doesn't add a please, and I feel both angry and disappointed. I am, after all, only trying to help.

Tamsin, the diplomat, steps in. "Thank you, Louisa. This all sounds very positive!"

The discussion moves on to the Christmas party. I normally shudder at the thought of these things, but I know this will be low-key, and I've become fond of many of my colleagues here at the food hub – particularly Tamsin. The intention is to run the usual food pantry in the morning, then hire the Saltings community space for the rest of the day, so people can drop in or stay for hours, as suits them.

"Maggie says she thinks we'll be able to have it for nothing, but she doesn't want to make any promises until she's spoken to Graham," Tamsin tells us.

"She's a wonderful woman," John says.

"Too young for you!" Mark grins and nudges him.

"I'm just saying..." John protests.

"She's an important contact for the hub," Jude says, "so there'll be no more of that talk, thank you, no matter how light-hearted you might consider it."

She glances at me then and I smile. She holds my gaze for a moment.

Jude goes on to say that I'm to shadow Tamsin that morning, too, with a view to taking on a Front of House position in the new year. I feel lifted again. I would never have imagined that a simple volunteering role would have raised such conflicting emotions in me. But I suppose I'm becoming invested in this place, and as painful as it is to admit it, I do care about what these people think of me.

I bump into Tamsin when I am leaving. She's outside, having a cigarette.

"I'm looking forward to working more closely with you," I tell her. "And to be honest I'm relieved Jude hasn't held it against me, pouring cold water on her fundraising ideas."

"Oh no – at least, I don't think so. I mean, Jude likes to be in charge – but she's a realist, and she will do anything for this place. If you can achieve in one meeting what she can via a squillion grant applications and sponsored swims, then she'll be happy."

"Are you sure? I'm still not convinced she likes me."

"She does. Trust me." Tamsin smiles and crumples her cigarette against the grid of the outside ashtray. I watch the still-glowing clump of ash drop to the ground.

"If she seems a bit down on everything, it's because it's a hard time of year for her," Tamsin continues, but doesn't expand any further on this. "Plus, she persuaded the board to reduce her salary in order to increase mine."

"She didn't!"

"She did. I didn't know anything about it. I'm still not entirely comfortable with it, but she insisted."

"Wow."

"I know."

I get in my car, thinking about Jude's generosity. And her dedication. She and I might not see eye to eye, but I have a growing respect for her. There is much that goes on behind the scenes, and I don't know the half of it. I just hope that with my suggestion I haven't been very stupid, and promised much more than I can deliver. Now that I know about the precarious nature of financing the hub, I am going to have to find a way to make this happen. Could I do what Jude does – give up some of my own money? I like to think so. But I couldn't do it forever, and besides, we are not at that point yet. Hopefully, we won't be at all. I wouldn't like my philanthropic capability to be tested.

I listen to a radio programme about a family stressed and scared by the forthcoming winter, and having to find the money to heat their home, on top of increasing food bills, not to mention Christmas presents. Then there are things like Christmas jumper days at school. With three children, that will be another outlay, and they have to pay another £1 each for the privilege of wearing them. It wasn't really done when Ada was at school, but I doubt I would have given it a second thought. Any extra expenses were never a problem for us. I worked very hard for that to be the case, but I am increasingly aware that there are very many people who also work incredibly hard, yet still are struggling to make ends meet. Listening to this family's story makes me all the more determined to make things work, for Tamsin, for Jude, and for everyone who needs the hub.

I explain my idea to Mum as we drive to the station to collect Ada.

"And would Tony be happy to help, do you think? Even after...?"

"Yes," I say quickly, to close down this line of conversation. I may have opened up to her, but I don't want to keep going on about it at every opportunity. "He would."

"He's a bit of a marvel, isn't he?"

"He's a good man, yes."

"Do you mind him being with Maggie?"

"No, Mum. You asked me that before, and my answer is the same. Why would I mind? They seem very well suited. And it's none of my business."

"I take my hat off to you all, to be honest."

"Well, life's too short, isn't it?"

This response is not something Mum would expect from me; it's not something I would normally expect myself to say, either. It must be the effect of the people I've been mixing with. I had come here expecting to dislike Maggie, and to feel uncomfortable around Tony, but they have been so open and welcoming, and they seem so genuinely happy and good together, that I can't feel anything but positivity towards them. It's the same with Tamsin, too, and the 'boys' in the depot – all the volunteers there, in fact (and even Jude, I'll grudgingly admit), not to mention the people that need us.

It's good to think of there being an 'us'. Me having a place here. Belonging. Did I ever feel like I belonged in London? I don't suppose I stopped to think about it. I was work, and work was me. I could have been anywhere. Having Ada rooted me, to some extent. I felt needed in a way I never had before. And now I feel needed again.

"Mum!" Ada says, throwing her arms around me and

then turning and doing the same to her grandmother. She has cut her hair shorter, and it's made it wavy. She's pierced her nose, too. She looks older (still decades younger than me, of course). But she looks wonderful.

"How was your journey?" I ask her, shouldering her bag and leading the way to the car park. I turn to see she has linked arms with my mum, who is practically skipping with happiness – she would be if she could.

"I just worked, to be honest, until we got to the sea – then I stopped working and gazed out of the window. I almost forgot to get off the train at St Erth!"

"Well, I'd have come to Penzance if you had." I wait a moment for them to catch up, then I switch the bag to my left arm and put my right around my daughter's shoulder. She is safely sandwiched between her mother and grandmother. As I consider this scene, I experience something which I can only describe as a sense of fullness. Contentment. All is well with the world. Our world, at least.

Ada splits her time between my place and Mum's. On Wednesday morning, I bring her up to the hub with me. Jude is very welcoming and seems taken with Ada, who has a way about her that I wish I could bottle.

I show Ada around, introducing her to my work 'family', as Tamsin calls us. I feel very proud – both of my daughter, and of being able to show her what I do these days.

"She's a lovely girl," Jude says to me.

"Thank you." I smile. "I don't know why I feel like I should say thank you. I've no right to claim any responsibility for her loveliness!"

"Oh, I think you do. At least, a little bit."

I look at her and I ask a question that years of carefully honed political correctness training should have banished from me: "Do you have any children?"

Immediately, I regret it. I see something pained in her expression. But she answers, matter-of-factly: "I do. I have two children. One living, one dead. He died when he was very young, but he is still my child."

"I'm so sorry," I say, feeling the weight of futility in those words. "And your..." What do I say? Living child? That sounds odd.

"My daughter. She's not much older than your Ada. She lives with her dad. Back in Devon."

"Oh, OK." Jude has never mentioned an ex before. She never mentions her love life at all, come to think of it – but then, neither do I. Largely because I don't have one.

"Do you see her?"

"Not often, no."

"That must be difficult."

"Yes. It is." She starts gathering up some empty food packaging, signalling the conversation is over. I help her, and we work companionably, sorting it into what can be recycled and what must be thrown away.

"Ada and I can take this to the recycling centre, if that helps," I say.

"It definitely would, thank you, Lou." Lou. Only my mum and Laurie call me that. I find I like it from Jude. It makes me feel a little bit more accepted. And then, she puts her hand on my arm and looks steadily into my eyes. "Thank you, for asking me about my family."

"Oh, well, that's quite alright. I didn't want to be intrusive."

"You weren't."

She heads off to her office, at the sound of the phone ringing, but she leaves me with a little glow, and I smile as I call across to Ada, to tell her that there's work to do.

We have dinner at Tregynon one night, with Maggie, Lucy and Stevie. Ada and Stevie are thick as thieves, showing each other videos on their phones, and taking selfies with silly filters on. They take one of me and Maggie, in Munch's *Scream* style. It is actually quite amusing.

I haven't seen Maggie since our day out at the Eden Project. "How's life been lately? Is Tony back in town?" I ask, taking a sip of my G&T.

"Yes, and it looks like he will be here for a while now," she smiles. She looks at me then. "Louisa..."

"Yes?" I think I know what's coming.

"He told me about... your history. I hope you don't mind."

"Did he? Well, no, I suppose he was bound to tell you some time. If you two are getting serious?"

"I think we are," she says, with a note of apology in her voice.

"Well, that's good. Really good. I'm pleased for you."

"Thank you."

"Genuinely. He's a good person. And I think you're well suited."

It's as close to a compliment as I can manage. Maggie's cheeks flush, so I think I have hit the right spot. "Have you told him about Sean?" I ask now.

Her cheeks glow redder, and she looks slightly panicked. "Sean?"

"Yes," I say gently. "I worked it out. It must be very difficult, him being here."

Her face has gone from flushed to pale. "Oh god, is it obvious?"

"Not obvious as such, but I think if I've pieced it together, it might not be long before other people do. Does your mum know?"

"No… not yet. I keep thinking I should tell her."

"Maybe you should. And he doesn't know?" I speak quietly, keeping half an eye on the others, but they are all engaged in their own conversations. What has happened to me? I have never been so nosy before. I've never really been all that interested in other people's lives, I suppose. Maybe it's just what happens when you live in a small town. But I'm genuinely concerned for Maggie. This is just the kind of thing which could blow up, if she's not careful. I know full well that these kind of things have a habit of catching up eventually.

"No. Well, I don't know. He might have worked it out." I think of the look Sean had given Stevie, when she spent the day with me. Perhaps he wasn't considering her relationship to me. Maybe he was thinking about her relationship to him.

"If he hasn't already, I think he will."

"That's what Elise said."

"So Mum knows?"

"Yes, I told her a while ago."

This needles me a little, although why should it? Their friendship is independent of me. Maybe what bothers me more is how much Mum has told Maggie in return. Has she confided more in Maggie than me?

"I'm surprised, though. He doesn't seem your type," I

say, not entirely kindly.

"No, well he's not, really. He caught me at a moment of weakness."

"I've certainly been there," I grimace.

"I think we all have. All us women, anyway."

I glance across at Ada, and I hope that things will be different for her.

"I'm sorry," I say.

"Don't be! I've got Stevie, haven't I? And I wouldn't have, if I hadn't..."

"Too true." I see Ada looking across at me, and I smile. "To our wonderful daughters," I proclaim loudly enough for the whole table to hear, raising a glass to Maggie's.

When Mum and Lucy echo the sentiment and toast each other, Maggie and I look at each other and smile.

The food arrives, and the chatter subsides for a while, but as we become increasingly full, and a little more relaxed, thanks to the wine (even Stevie is allowed a small glass), our table becomes increasingly loud, and our little corner of the restaurant rings with laughter.

I think back to the slightly awkward meal I had here with Mum, when I'd just moved back. How different this is. In time, though, I can see she looks tired, and I remind myself that she is still getting over the illness.

"Are you worrying about her?" Maggie asks me.

"Who, Mum? No, she'll outlive me," I smile but then, touched by her noticing, I admit, "Well, I am a little. That bug has knocked her. Although she's trying very hard not to let us see it."

"I'll get Tony to give her a lift back. He's coming to collect me and Mum and Stevie. But he won't be able to squeeze you and Ada in, I'm really sorry."

"That is quite alright! We're more than equal to the walk home. Thank you, though. And listen, if you ever want to talk, let me know."

"I will. I might. Thanks. It's a relief, in a way, you knowing. There's only Julia, as well as you and your mum, who knows the truth."

"You can trust me, I promise."

"I know that."

On the way back to my place, Ada links arms with me, as she had with Mum the other day.

"What a great evening!"

I squeeze her arm with mine. "I love you so much."

"I love you, too."

The air is cold and crisp, and very still – just a whisper of a breeze tickles the back of my neck, producing something close to a shiver. There is no cloud cover, so the stars glimmer and glint above us, and the moonlight falls pleasingly across the sea. My daughter and I walk companionably back towards the town, and my thoughts turn to Jude, estranged from her girl, and forever grieving her boy. I ache for her, and it makes me pull Ada closer to me.

"I do," I say. "I love you more than you could ever know."

"Mum!" Ada says fondly, all her life ahead of her, and no idea what it feels like to be a parent – to love so fiercely, and for your worst fear to be anything bad ever happening to your child. I could never have imagined feeling like this, before I had her.

I laugh. I'm glad for her. It's how it should be, right now. There is time enough.

We take the stairs up to my apartment, with Ada's long legs striding confidently and quickly up. But I am not far behind – I've done this so many times now, I've built up a steady fitness and strength, and my breathing is far easier than it was in those early days living here.

When we reach the space outside my front door, we hear the lift ping. I experience a familiar sinking feeling, and sure enough, out comes Stacey.

"Hi Louise!" she says. Her eyes fall on Ada. "Is this your daughter?"

"Yes, this is Ada."

Ada smiles and shakes Stacey's hand. She is so bloody lovely to everyone.

"It must be nice to have a daughter. I've just got my three boys. You know what they're like. Well, no, you probably don't!" She laughs at her own words. "Anyway, we've got some news, actually." Her face displays a kind of mock-sadness. She pouts her bottom lip out.

"Oh?"

"Yes, we're moving on."

"Really?" I try to suppress the joy.

"Yes, I'm afraid so. Sean's got himself a new job, back up north."

"Really?"

"Yes, in Leeds. It's another promotion, so…"

"Well, congratulations to him. And to you."

"Thanks. I'm excited about it!"

She doesn't sound particularly excited.

"He didn't tell me he was going for it," she says conspiratorially. "He's quite a career chaser, though. I suppose most men are… not like us girls, eh?"

Ada looks at me, but I just smile.

"Quite. So are you selling up?" I ask.

"Oh, no, we're changing our mortgage to a buy-to-let."

"Of course you are." Soon, then, I will be the only resident here, and subject to the comings and goings of holiday-makers.

"We can come back for holidays ourselves! Although Sean says he wants us to start going abroad. Says he fancies those all-inclusive deals."

"They do sound good," I agree. "Anyway, we'd better get in. Congratulations again." It's a bit mean, but I can't bring myself to say I am sorry they are leaving. I want to call Maggie and tell her the news. It will certainly make her life a bit easier. Although I still think that secrets like that are impossible to keep forever.

2021

When Tony and Samantha returned from one of their trips to Cornwall, it was clear that AJ and Louisa did not have the monopoly on work relationships. Although nothing was said, something had changed, in the way they looked at each other, and spoke to each other. Besides, Louisa had seen them holding hands on the way into work. She had hung back, watching from a little way back on the other side of the road as they kissed and parted ways – Tony walking around the block while Samantha went ahead to the office, so as not to arrive together. Louisa might previously have disapproved, which was hypocritical enough considering her history, but now she knew she didn't have a leg to stand on.

Besides, she liked Tony. And she actually liked Samantha. In fact, she found her very easy to get on with, in a way she rarely did with other women. Or with men, come to think of it. But there sometimes seemed to be some kind of expectation when it came to her relationships with the handful of women in the office. Since Teresa had left – she had stayed on another fifteen years after the day Gianni died, but decided to retire when Gerald Lacey did (prompting lots of smutty jokes about the nature of their relationship) – Louisa couldn't think of anyone at work who she would count as a friend. While it might have been anticipated that, as the most senior woman in the company, she would want to help others follow her lead, aside from a couple of exceptions she considered worthy of her time, if anything, she was harsher towards her female colleagues than the men.

She had heard all the arguments, and criticisms, of

course. Women at her level had to be aggressive, to get to where they were. They needed to be twice as macho as the men, and twice as mean. Most women at work assumed Louisa didn't have children and they were surprised to hear about Ada. Even more surprised if they actually met her, and discovered that she was the polar opposite of the stuck-up, obnoxious child they had expected Louisa to produce.

But Samantha was different. She was straightforward. Confident. Direct. Maybe it was because she was a client rather than a colleague. Louisa had to begin their relationship differently. But actually, they just really seemed to hit it off. Samantha – Sammie – was lively, and fun, and intellectually interesting. She was well read and politically engaged. Louisa liked to discuss the difference between American and British politics with Sammie, while AJ would back away, saying all politicians were the same.

"That's a load of bollocks," Louisa said, knowing that he would get a kick out of such a British swear word. "They are not all the same. Even if you think none of them can be trusted. They are certainly not all self-interested. Look at the women out there. Do you know how much abuse they receive, on a daily basis? Online and in the mail, death threats, rape threats, commentary on their looks, their bodies, their clothes... And they might earn a decent wage, but it's not nearly as much as you can make in an industry like ours, if you put your mind to it. So what are they getting out of it, really? They must believe in what they're doing. Otherwise, why put themselves through all of that shit?"

This was late one night, when the four of them –

Louisa, AJ, Sammie and Tony – had gone for a Chinese meal after finishing work well after nine. The MSG would play havoc with her stomach overnight, but Louisa loved Chinese food. She also loved spending time with these three, she realised. Tony was kind and considerate and easy-going. Sammie was lively, outgoing, and a lot of fun. AJ was tall, handsome, and incredibly charming. Her skin tingled at the thought of the previous night, when she'd gone to see him in his hotel after hours. Ada had been at Clara's, so Louisa was in no rush to get back. And AJ had made it clear he'd like her to come and visit him.

They had lain in bed for some time, and the conversation had turned to Cornwall, as it often did.

"Why don't you come and visit with me?" she had asked him, almost shyly.

"What, Cornwall?" He'd pushed himself up onto his elbow. "I'd love to."

"Really?"

"Of course! I mean, I have to go there again anyway, for work. But I would love for you to show me around."

"I'm planning a trip in a few weeks," she had said, although she hadn't actually planned anything. She hoped it would be alright with Elise, but couldn't think that her mother would have anything too pressing to make it a problem. "For an actual week away from work. Do you think you could come down at the weekend?"

"Sure. Why don't I say Thursday? That way I can put it on my expenses," he had twinkled.

"And maybe you could come and say hello to my mum?" She found the conversation toe-curlingly awkward, and now she was making such a teenage suggestion. They

were both of them too old to 'meet the parents'. But
Louisa wanted to show Elise that she was not just a
dreadful, dried-up career woman. It might offer her
mum some reassurance, as she clearly worried that
Louisa would end up alone and, worse, lonely. As if Elise
was anyone to talk! On top of all that, though, Louisa
had met somebody that she really liked, and she was
excited about it. She wanted to share it with her mum.
Even in her early sixties, Louisa realised that she still
craved her mother's approval.

She also wanted AJ to meet Ada – or Ada to meet AJ –
but that could wait, until after the visit to Cornwall.

Louisa

On the morning of the Christmas party, I get an outfit ready for later on – nothing much, just a nice pair of trousers and a top, and my favourite pair of boots, but for now I put on the jeans I bought in Next, and my trainers. I'm not quite used to wearing them, or at least I am not used to my reflection in the mirror. I find myself wondering what Jude will think of me dressing like this. The trousers and shoes are certainly practical. And comfortable. However, I am not one of those people who believe that comfort is everything, and I like to make an effort with my appearance. The day I stop doing that is the beginning of the end.

All I have to do is go downstairs, once the community space is open. I go early, and I am the first customer of the day in the café, where I buy coffees and pastries for Jude and Tamsin. Today, as well as the food and general supplies, the Pantry has a whole bank of children's toys, hats, scarves and gloves, and lovely toiletries – the product of some extra funding from Canyon. After I spoke to him, Tony managed to convince them to increase their budget for next year, so Tamsin and Jude can both be paid fully for full-time jobs (although this still has to be signed off, so Jude has not shared the news with Tamsin yet), but also to provide a 'Christmas bonus' for the hub here. The donations in the office in London were already earmarked for local people – it's not just the Cornish who are struggling.

"Louisa!" Tamsin says, grinning at the sight of her custard crown, and taking a sip of her much-too-sweet (in my opinion) caramel macchiato.

"Oh my god, I need this today!" Jude says. She has a black coffee, and a plain croissant. I note her make-up is a bit brighter than normal, with some sparkly eyeshadow. Tamsin has gone the whole hog and has tinsel in her hair, and some kind of glitter adorning her cheekbones. They are in the process of decking out the space beautifully, too. There are paper chains, scooping up and down around the room, taking me back to primary school. There is an artificial tree in the corner, which Tamsin is currently adorning with baubles, and around the bank of presents-in-waiting is tinsel. Behind it, the wall is swathed in white sheets, which somebody has painted with a wintry forest scene. It's pretty impressive – snow-topped fir trees, one with a deer hiding behind it, one with an owl sitting amid its branches. I'm just admiring it when Jude comes up and hands me a tub. "Can you help me throw this at the sheets, Lou?"

"What is this? Glitter?"

"Yes. Bio-degradable, of course."

"Of course." I hadn't even thought that might be a possibility.

"I'm sorry it will get all over you!"

"That's fine, I've got my party clothes ready!" I smile. "Are you getting changed here?"

"Oh... no, this is me," she says, with a little gesture towards herself. She is wearing a cardigan, but underneath that is a close-fitting dark red top with a scoop neck that shows off her collarbone, and she is also wearing some skinny jeans, and boots.

"I'm so sorry! I can see that now." Am I actually blushing?

"It's fine!" she laughs. "I'm normally a scruffy bugger, so me dressing up is most people's idea of normal."

"Well, you look lovely."

"Thank you," she smiles, and I think I detect a little glow across her cheeks, too. She doesn't comment on my new clothes, and I wonder whether she has even noticed. I'm sure she's got more important things to worry about than what her volunteers are wearing. But I realise I had hoped she would have seen, and approved. What is happening to me?

Jude sprays the sheets with water, and I throw the glitter where she has sprayed. It works – it sticks! Or most of it does... however, where it falls to the floor looks just as festive.

"Let's get the music on!" Tamsin calls, and soon the room is filled with cheery Christmas songs. I actually have always found this kind of music grates on me. Especially when the shops have it playing from the start of November onwards. I prefer traditional carols, or orchestral pieces, but I have to concede there is a place for Christmas cheer.

Soon, the room is bright and festive, and we are ready to go. I take a seat next to Tamsin, and we wait for the first 'clients' (we still haven't thought of an appropriate alternative) of the day.

It isn't long. A tentative knock on the door, and in come a young couple, with a baby in a pushchair. Jude welcomes them, and I see her putting her hand on the woman's arm as she talks to her quietly, then guiding them across first to the bank of presents, and then on to the food. In January, we will be trialling the warm hub, offering people blankets, and hats and gloves – slow cookers, and hot-water bottles. "It's an absolute disgrace in this country that we have to do this," Jude has fumed, more than once. "That we've come to accept places like this as part of the fabric of society. People seem to have forgotten the government's responsibility to take care of people, not leave them floundering and reliant on charity. We are not a poor country, but the number of families living in poverty. And it's not just the people on benefits – not that needing support is anything to be ashamed of – but there's plenty of people who work coming in these days."

While I had begun here without any particular political interest, I have by now seen and heard enough to be able to see her point.

The room is soon buzzing, as some of the other hub family arrive to help distribute goods, and there is no shortage of people who need our help.

Tamsin is able to provide practical advice for seeking help with benefits, tax credits, and childcare costs, and I sit feeling like a bit of a spare part, but taking notes on my laptop, which I can print off or email and share with the people we are helping, and which I can also use for my own benefit, to begin to learn what is out there, and what people need.

We run for a full four hours today, and it is no

exaggeration to say that there is not a quiet moment. It is always difficult as we approach cut-off time. If anybody is late, how do you turn them away? I watch Jude usher in a lady who looks very awkward, but Jude guides her smoothly around the place, explaining how it all works, and even managing to make the woman laugh.

The supplies greatly diminished, we shut the door, and begin to pile up everything that is left, along with the shelving and empty crates. Matthew and Mark have already arrived, with the van, and they carry out any excess – not that there is much – and then bring in our Christmas party food, and a box of games. Including Twister, I note with trepidation.

"Are you going up to get changed?" Jude asks me.

"Oh, erm..." I'd all but forgotten about that. Everyone is dressed casually, although many are wearing Christmas jumpers with their jeans. Should I stick with what I'm wearing? No. "I'll just nip up to the flat," I say. I may be settling into this new world, but I am still me.

I rush to get my clothes on, not wanting to take too long and miss out on the fun. Still, I root through my make-up bag for something suitably festive. I clip my hair up and apply some sparkly eye make-up, then I put on some lipstick, but a look in the mirror has me rubbing it off. I don't want to be too over-the-top.

Back downstairs, I find Jude has produced six bottles of prosecco, and she's popped a couple open. Tamsin hands me a glass. "Cheers, Louisa."

"Cheers!" I note that Jude just has a glass of water. I wish she would let her hair down, but I respect how seriously she takes her responsibility.

"I bet this all seems a bit lame compared to the glamorous work parties you're used to!" Tamsin says.

"I hated them!" I admit. "I'd normally find an excuse to avoid them – usually work!" An image drifts into my mind of Gianni watching me put sandwiches and tomatoes on my plate. Him joining me to eat, as though it didn't matter what anybody else thought.

"Ah, that's a shame."

"Not really. It was a very male workplace. And it never felt more so than at social events."

"That sounds pretty awful!"

"In many ways it was quite good, working there, once you got past the smutty comments and visible adjusting of testicles through suit trousers. Or the assumption that it's OK to put your arm around a female colleague when you're showing her something on a computer."

Tamsin shudders but laughs.

"There at least was not the kind of gossip and bitchiness you might find in a more female-oriented workplace."

Tamsin considers this. "So you'd rather work with men than women?"

"Not necessarily. It depends on the woman," I say, looking across at Jude chatting to Daisy and Mandy, who do some of the deliveries to the very rural areas, for people who can't easily get out and about on their own.

"Well, I'm glad you're here, with us. You're becoming indispensable. Jude was singing your praises the other day."

"Was she?"

"Oh yeah, I think she's taken a shine to you."

"I think she thinks I'm shallow and materialistic."

"Why?"

"Because I am!" I laugh, and Tamsin does too.

2021

When Louisa mentioned to Elise that she was coming 'home' for a few days, the delight was clear in her mother's voice. There was also relief in her voice and Louisa realised that Elise had been worried – clearly surprised to receive a call from her daughter in the middle of the day. It made Louisa feel guilty, knowing she didn't speak to her mum enough. Just a perfunctory call or two a week, normally started with 'I can't stay on long...'

"Hello? Love?"

"Hi, Mum." Louisa was vaguely aware of a siren on a nearby street, and the beep of a horn. She imagined her mum feeling grateful she didn't have to live in a city like London. But to Louisa, these sounds were a comfort. Signs of life. She remembered the quiet of the locked-down London, when the Covid pandemic was at its worst. The city had felt so stripped back and almost sinister. Like something terrible was imminent – although of course it was already happening. There were still sirens then, and many of them, with precious little traffic to dilute their urgent cries. The sound had been close to panic-inducing then.

"Hi, Louisa. How are you?" Elise sounded a little more settled now.

"I'm fine, Mum. Are you?"

"Yes, thanks. A bit tired today, you know."

"Well, make sure you rest, then."

"It's all I ever do!" Elise laughed. "Now, aren't you meant to be at work?"

"Yes, I am, I've just stepped out for a bit. It's a

beautiful day." She was aware this was out of character for her – the phone call, the stepping out of work. No matter how beautiful a day it may be. "I just wanted to see how you are, Mum. And to let you know I'm coming to Cornwall in a few weeks."

"Really?" The surprise and delight were obvious, even down a phone line. Louisa did not need to see her mother's face to know she was smiling.

"Yes, I thought... I thought maybe we could spend some time together. You know, I might come for a week. Maybe more."

"OK..." A pause. "Is everything OK?"

Louisa just laughed. "Yes, Mum, everything's fine. I'm fine. I just... I know we haven't spent a lot of time together lately, and I miss you, and I miss Cornwall, I suppose. It's been hard at work lately and I can't think of anywhere I'd rather be." She leaves out the part about work being all tied up in Cornwall these days. Elise could not seem to get her head around the fact that Louisa is involved in the Saltings development yet not an employee of Canyon Holdings. Louisa knows it will irritate her if they go down that route again. And this is meant to be a positive call. Good news, for once. At least she hopes her mum sees it that way.

"Well, my love, you know you're welcome any time, and you know I'd love to see you. Your room's always ready for you. Well, unless Ada's visiting, of course!"

It made Louisa smile, that she had been usurped by her daughter. She knew Ada was a better granddaughter than she was a daughter. And she was about to prove it. She took a breath. "Oh thanks, Mum, but I think I'll stay in the hotel."

"Oh." Elise was disappointed. But Louisa did not want to stay in her childhood bedroom – for a whole host of reasons. Not just because Tregynon offered large, luxurious bedrooms and super-fast WiFi.

"You don't mind, do you?"

"No, no, of course I don't." And actually, Elise found that she really didn't mind. Her daughter was coming home. Just for a week. But – a whole week!

Hotel or not, she couldn't help but feel delighted.

***

It was a fresh Saturday morning in Cornwall, and the clocks were turning forward that night. Elise had risen with the sun, too excited to sleep any longer. She was up and out early, down at the weekly farmer's market, buying fresh bread, cheese, pickles and olives for lunch. All things her daughter loved. She popped into Bramley's for a small Victoria sponge, which was always Louisa's favourite, and Bramley's did the best in town.

On the other side of the country, just a couple of hundred miles away, Louisa was driving west, humming to herself. Life felt good in a way that it hadn't for quite some time. She thought of AJ and how he made her feel. Determined though she was that no man would have such an effect on her again, this had crept up on her. She was no fool. She knew he reminded her of Gianni. The accent, the self-assuredness. Her old love had left an imprint on her heart and soul, and body – of what a man should be. Or at least if he was to deserve any piece of Louisa Morgan's heart.

She stopped at a service station, noting the beautiful

blue sky above the dull, flat building, packed car park and litter-strewn hedges and pathways. One over-priced coffee later, she was ready to go. She took a moment to send two messages.

To AJ: **I'm on my way! Looking forward to showing you around my old patch. Lxx**

Obscure detail though it may be, she knew she had not signed off any communication in that manner since Gianni. She even remembered that last email she sent him, which went unanswered. Despite her subsequent discovery of him as a married man and cheat, some part of her still ached for him, and his far-too-early death. And for what might have been. Who knew what state his marriage was in? Perhaps his wife didn't understand him, she thought to herself with a wry grin. More likely he was just having his cake and eating it. But she knew that she hadn't imagined the chemistry between them. She was sure she hadn't. She just could not believe that he had been with her purely because she was an easy route to infidelity. A convenient bedmate in London when he was feeling horny.

For one thing, he was risking his position at work. Although... was he really? Didn't men get away with that sort of thing all the time? The thought sat uncomfortably with her, aware of how her relationship with AJ might be perceived. For one thing, he was a client. For another, he was younger than her. Now, any man worth his salt would let these things roll off him like water off a duck's back, but Louisa had worked so incredibly hard, stayed so incredibly straight, to get to where she was. The topmost echelons of her company were almost exclusively male, and unlikely to approve of her relationship with a younger man. A client. AJ's boss at Canyon was a man as well. He might do a bit of wink, wink, nudge, nudge kind of stuff with AJ, but it was unlikely to put Louisa in a strong position.

She pushed the thoughts away. What was she meant to do? Become a nun? Ada was always telling her she should try to find somebody, but that sounded too much like hard work. She wasn't going to get on one of those dating apps and swipe past a hundred men only to find the one that she matched with had put on a photo from twenty years ago and neglected to mention his criminal record and/or foot fetish.

To Elise: **Roads are clear and I'm on my way! See you soon, Mum xx**

***

Something about that 'Mum' in Louisa's message made Elise's heart sing. At eleven o'clock, she was on her feet, in the kitchen, the kettle and radio on and the back door open, birdsong filtering into her house. At 11.28, there was the sound of a key in the door and Elise turned to hear her daughter's voice:

"Hi, Mum!"

Hi, Mum! It's what Louisa would call when she came home from school – Laurie, too. Elise had missed it. Missed those days, even though they had seemed hard work at the time. Keeping uniforms clean; making sure both children had shoes that fitted; trying to scrape together the money for the occasional school trip; keeping up with homework.

She met Louisa halfway, in the lounge, aware of her shrinking body, as her daughter now appeared to tower above her. They both had smiles on their faces as they embraced, and Louisa kissed her mother's cheek, then tried a surreptitious examination of her, checking for signs of illness. Elise pretended not to notice.

"It is so nice to see you, Lou," Elise said. "You look well."

Louisa really did look well. Her dark hair was glossy, and for once a little messy; her cheeks pink and her brown eyes shining.

"I walked down from the hotel," she said. "I thought it made sense to leave the car there."

"Oh, yes, I suppose it does. There's not much in the way of parking round here, that's for sure. Did you have a good journey? Would you like a cup of tea?"

"I'd love one, please, Mum. And could we have it in the garden? It's just so nice to be in so much fresh air. I want to make the most of every moment of it."

"Of course we can."

Although she had planned to save the cake for after lunch, Elise decided to get it out straightaway, bringing a big wedge for her daughter to enjoy with her steaming mug of tea.

"From Bramley's?" Louisa asked.

"Of course."

"This is too good. Thank you, Mum."

"It's my pleasure."

Louisa wanted to offer to go and fetch Elise's, but knew her mum well enough to realise it wouldn't go down well. Instead, she sat back in the striped lounger and took a big bite of her cake, making Elise smile. She would like to take a walk with her daughter later, around town. Visit some of their favourite old spots. Treat Louisa to an ice-cream. But something – the fear of being knocked back – stopped her from suggesting this.

They sat companionably for a while, watched closely by a gull strutting slowly back and forth across the low roof at the back of the house, its almost orange eyes fixed on their plates.

"How are you, Mum? The garden's looking nice." This felt too polite to Louisa. Like she was just making small talk with somebody she barely knew.

"I'm really quite well, thank you, love. The garden keeps me busy, and I've been going to the club a bit more."

"Caring the Community?" Louisa hated the name as much as Elise did and she grinned suddenly.

"That's the one. And there's a lovely girl... woman –" Elise quickly corrected herself, knowing Louisa would if she didn't – "who volunteers there, and she's taken me out a couple of times, with her daughter."

Elise looked at Louisa. She felt a little awkward about her friendship with Maggie, who had been mistaken for her daughter more than once, although in truth she was young enough to be Elise's granddaughter.

But Louisa just said, "That's really nice. I'm glad you've got some company, Mum." She paused, and it was clear to Elise that Louisa was thinking more of something she wanted to talk about than any new friend of her mother's. "Actually, Mum, I've had some more company lately, too."

"Oh yes?"

"Yes, I've got a… a boyfriend, I suppose." *Cringe*, as Ada would say. Surely Louisa was too old to have a boyfriend, for goodness' sake. But 'partner' made it sound like she and AJ had committed to each other for life.

"Really?"

"Yes, although we haven't been seeing each other long."

"Well, he must be nice if you're telling me about him."

Louisa's face flushed. "He is nice. He's from work, actually. And you know I don't normally mix work and pleasure. Not when it comes to relationships, anyway."

Elise nodded encouragingly, keen to hear more, actually thinking she had no idea about Louisa's love life, as she never normally told her a thing.

"But we get on really well. He came over from America last year, and we've been working closely together, and… we just clicked, I suppose."

"And he is single?" Elise kicked herself for the stupidity of this question.

"Mum!" Thankfully, Louisa just laughed. "Of course he is. He's been married, no kids. And he's quite a bit younger than me, actually."

"Oh really? Has Ada met him?"

"No, not yet, but she knows about him."

"And can I ask his name?"

"Yes, he's called AJ. Well, that's not his real name, but everyone at work calls him by his initials, and it seems to suit him, really."

"AJ. Sounds very American!"

"I suppose it does, quite! Anyway, strangely enough, he knows this place quite well. He's been seconded to work at our place, but actually works for Canyon Holdings. You know, the place behind the development at the harbour." How many times had she just said 'place'? It was nerves, she knew, from introducing this topic to her mum. She wanted to rush to the key part.

"The Saltings? That's quite a coincidence."

"I suppose it is. I couldn't believe it when he was talking about our little town. He really loves it here. In fact, he might come down this week, too."

Elise shot a quick, sharp look at her daughter. So this was why she'd been so keen to come. Still, she told herself, what mattered was that Louisa was here, now. And she was actually opening up to her. Elise had no idea who Ada's father was. She had no idea if Louisa had boyfriends... girlfriends, even. Not a clue. So surely this, now, was progress.

"So I'll get to meet him?"

"Maybe," Louisa smiled coyly.

It made Elise smile, too. "Louisa, if he makes you happy, then I already like him. And if he does come down this week, you can bring him here, if you'd like to. Or we can go out, if you'd rather."

"I'd like that, Mum."

"Now, shall we have some lunch? And–" Elise decided to chance it – "I wondered if you'd like to spend the afternoon with me. I thought we could walk along to the harbour, get a cup of tea and an ice cream somewhere. Just spend some time together." She hoped she didn't sound too desperate.

"I'd like that, Mum," Louisa said again.

It made Elise's heart swell.

***

Each day, Louisa woke up to the sound of the gulls – they struck her as more wholesome than those in London, somehow, even though she knew full well that they were expert ice-cream thieves and stealers of chips. She checked her phone for messages, and checked her emails. She was keeping an eye on developments for work, she told herself, knowing full well she was actually desperate to hear from AJ.

He'd sent a couple of texts when she first got there, but had not responded to her latest message. She was not so desperate as to step in and contact him again. And she knew he was busy. She had just discovered (via Tim, her PA) that the following week, AJ's overlords, as he called them, would be in London. The team – Louisa, AJ, Samantha and Tony – were presenting their work to the board, ready for approval. They also were expected to eat out with the Canyon CEO and COO on Monday night. It made Louisa nervous; not a feeling she was generally accustomed to. It really would have helped to have heard more from AJ. Still, she would be seeing him soon enough. And Sammie, at least, had kept in touch, surprisingly regularly:

I'm missing you here, L. Just me and the boys xxx

Louisa had been surprised and flattered by this.

I'll be back soon enough.

She couldn't bring herself to add a kiss. It would be out of character for her. But then she thought her response was too sharp. Did it sound rude rather than reassuring?

But Sammie's reply suggested she had not been put off.

Maybe we can spend some time in Cornwall together one day! No boys xxx

I'd like that.

Louisa hadn't wanted her mum to think that the trip was about work, but as the nerves set in about the following week's presentation, she couldn't help but mention it.

"I'm going to have a lot to do next week."

"I'm sure. Try and put it out of your mind this week, though." Elise was well aware that she sounded like somebody who had no idea about Louisa's world. How all-consuming it was.

"It's not that easy, Mum." Louisa's irritation was evident, but she didn't want it to come out like that.

"I know, I'm sorry. I don't suppose you can just forget about it. It's a shame you haven't got two weeks down here. I always think it takes a week to unwind, before you can really feel like you're relaxed."

"Two weeks would be lovely, but it's just not… Tim says there's a meeting on Monday that I won't even have prepared for, unless I work over the weekend."

"You've heard from Tim, then?"

"Oh, er, yes, I… anyway, like you said, better to try and put it out of my mind. I'll just have to work late on Sunday."

"That's a shame." Elise found the words she had wanted to say for some time: "I'm proud of you, Louisa."

"Are you?" Louisa looked up at her mother.

"Yes, my darling, I'm really proud of you, and I always have been. God knows, I have no idea what you actually do–" Elise laughed and so did Louisa – "but bloody hell, Lou, you obviously do it well."

"Thank you, Mum," Louisa said softly, and hugged Elise. Even though they were at the harbour, in public, they stood and held each other firmly, each trying to convey the strength of their feelings for the other.

The following day was leisurely and relaxed for Elise – less so for Louisa, who had got up early to do some work and thereafter was trying very hard not to think too much about the forthcoming presentation, or about AJ, and instead to make the most of her time with her mother. They had tea and doughnuts at Bramley's, then picked up some books from the charity shop and sat together in Elise's quiet little lounge, lost in the worlds of their books but also both well aware of the real world and the space they were occupying together in a way they hadn't for decades.

Later, they took a walk on the beach before tea, and Louisa cooked for them both before setting up a video call with Ada and Laurie.

Elise, feeling brave, ventured, "Wouldn't it be nice if we could all be together in person? Before too long."

"That would be amazing, Gran," Ada's beautiful young face smiled.

"I'd be up for that," Laurie said.

"Me too," agreed Louisa.

"Really?"

"Of course, Gran!" Ada laughed. "What about the summer? Or Christmas?"

"I could do Christmas," Laurie smiled. He looked younger than his close-to-seventy years, but his grey hair and weather-beaten face were clues to his age. And Louisa thought they suited him. Ageing seemed to work in her brother's favour. As he had become older, it seemed he had come more and more to be himself.

"I'm sure I can, too." Louisa smiled at Laurie, connecting via the screen. "And in the meantime, Mum, I'll be back more often. I plan to do this far more regularly."

Elise could scarcely believe it and she told herself not to count her chickens. But Louisa would not have said that if she hadn't meant it. None of them would. It looked like Christmas this year was going to be something to look forward to rather than just got through.

After the call, Louisa and Elise had a small whisky nightcap and then a hug, and Louisa said it: "I love you, Mum." Then she whirled out of the door and into the still, dark night.

When Louisa got back to the hotel, she took her phone from her bag. She saw she had a missed call, from AJ, and a voicemail. Without bothering to listen to the message, she called him back.

"Louisa."

"Hello handsome!" She was feeling happy and flippant, and determined to let everyone she cared about know how she felt.

"You sound happy."

"I am!"

"Did you listen to my message?"

"No." Her stomach dropped.

"Ah. I'm so sorry, but I'm not coming to Cornwall."

Louisa

After the buffet is all but finished, and the bottles are empty, Jude surprises us with a gift for each of us. Mine is a set of organic skincare bottles.

"Jude!" I find her later. "Thank you. I haven't got you anything," I confess.

"I didn't expect you to."

"Well, can I help clear up this place?" I ask, noting many of the volunteers have said their goodbyes and left.

"Sure. If you've time."

"I have."

"Tamsin, you get going." Jude smiles at her younger colleague. "Go on. You've been an enormous help, and you've worked your socks off. Not just today, but all year."

"Thank you, Jude." Tamsin gives her manager a hug and Jude looks surprised but pleased. I understand. It's tough being in charge. You have to stay at arm's length from your colleagues. It can be lonely.

When Tamsin has gone, I switch off the Christmas music. "I hope you don't mind?" I say to Jude.

"My god, no, it's a relief."

She opens one of the windows, and now we can hear the sounds of the harbour – the gulls, and the sea, and the shouts of some of the fishermen, a little way down the harbourside.

"What are your plans for Christmas?" I ask her.

"Oh, not much… I try to get out for a good long walk with the dog. Makes the day go quicker."

"You don't spend it with any family?" I am not sure I've phrased this correctly, knowing what I do about her children. "Siblings? Cousins? Friends?"

"No, sadly they're all a long way from here. My sister's in Australia, and most of my cousins are in the north-west, where my family's from. They've all got their own kids and in-laws and all that, anyway. It's fine, though. What about you, Lou?"

I feel bad telling her about our plans, which couldn't be more different. Ada and Laurie are both coming to stay – Ada with me, and Laurie with Mum. And we've told Mum we're having Christmas dinner at my place, but actually we have booked a table at Tregynon, along with Maggie, Stevie, Tony, Lucy, and Maggie's sister Julia and her family. I've always felt like Christmas should be a quietish affair; the one time of year when it really does feel acceptable to just stay in and do nothing. I could never have imagined I'd be looking forward to it becoming a social occasion. Yet here we are. I am, however, looking forward to spending some time with just my mum, my brother and my daughter, though. Back in the little house on Godolphin Terrace. Like Christmases used to be so long ago (although there was no Ada then, of course).

I'm excited about seeing Laurie, and I'm excited about Mum having us all together. I know how much it means to her.

I try to play this all down to Jude, though. I almost

want to ask her to join us, but I think that may be a step too far, and I don't think she would accept, anyway. She's a proud woman, just like me.

"It sounds like you've got a lovely Christmas planned," she says generously, handing me one end of one of the sheets, while she takes the other. We fold it up neatly, then do the same with the others.

When the place is packed up, I help her load everything into her car.

She is about to go, but I'd like her to stay a bit longer. "Would you like a drink?" I ask.

"Oh, well, erm, I'm driving..."

"OK. Maybe another time. I was thinking up at my place, though. I can make you a coffee if you like."

She looks at me, and smiles. "That would be lovely. Thank you, Lou."

I don't make Jude take the stairs with me – instead, we get in the elevator, and as the doors close, I feel a little awkward.

We are quiet for a while and then Jude says, "Do you know what? I could do with a drink! It's been a long year. I can leave my car here. Get a taxi later. As long as I'm not keeping you from anything."

"Not at all," I say. "I can either stay awake and keep on drinking, or have a nap!"

Jude laughs.

"Gin and tonic?" I suggest.

"Perfect."

Jude gazes out of the window at the view, while I pour us two generous G&Ts with thick, juicy chunks of lemon, imported very unsustainably for festive drinks. I feel self-conscious, aware of the luxury of this place, while having no idea where Jude lives. Perhaps she has a beautiful old town house. I can picture her in a cosy, muted place with books and a little stylish clutter. A kitchen with herbs on the windowsill, and her dog curled contentedly on a bed in the corner. Then again, maybe she lives in a flat, or a caravan. It's an expensive place to live, Cornwall. Knowing what I do about her sacrificing some of her salary for Tamsin, I guess Jude isn't on a huge wage.

"Cheers," I say, bringing the glasses over.

"Cheers," she says, smiling. "This is some place. I knew it would be. And I did have some sneaky peeks at the estate agent pictures when these flats went on the market."

So she'll know how much this apartment cost. I can't feel awkward, though. I've worked hard to get here. I can't be embarrassed. This is me.

"I suppose this development wasn't looked on hugely favourably," I say, gesturing towards my leather sofa, and Jude obligingly takes a seat. I place my glass on a coaster, and fetch some pistachios and a couple of bowls from the kitchen then sit down next to her.

"Well, no," Jude says, pulling off her boots and tucking her legs under her, making herself at home. I like it. "That won't be news to you, though."

"No," I admit, thinking back to the wrangles that we had with local groups, in the early stages. I empty the nuts into one of the bowls, and take a handful,

"Still, at least this one's gone to somebody local!" she laughs.

"I'm not sure I count as that these days."

"I don't know. I've been here about thirteen years, but I reckon I'm still regarded as an incomer. You can just waltz back in, and say you were born here. You've got your mum saving your place for you as well." She takes a long sip of her drink and sighs appreciatively. "That is good. Thank you."

"You're very welcome." I lift my glass and clink it against hers. "Mum's been here eighty years – she was born in London – but she says she's still considered an incomer. I think she's exaggerating, though. She's part and parcel of the place. And so are you. Look at everything you do for the community."

"I guess. Is it good being back?" She drops a handful of pistachio shells into the empty bowl.

"It is. It was strange at first. I'm so glad I found your hub. It's given me some focus. It takes some acclimatising, going from seventy-hour weeks to zero."

"Do you miss it?"

"The seventy-hour weeks? No!" I laugh. "But I did, at first. Just the feeling of purpose. Of there always being something to do. I may have moaned about it, but it filled my life. At any time, I could pull out my laptop and find something that required my input. There is definitely something in feeling needed."

"You must have felt that with Ada, as well?"

"I did," I smile. "I really did, although I did use a childminder as well," I say, as though confessing some terrible crime. "I had to, or I'd have lost my place at work. Some man, with a wife at home to look after his kids, would have easily slipped past me."

Jude grimaces.

"I don't think Ada suffered for it," I say.

"I am sure she didn't. And it's good for her, to see you working, and successful. Honestly. My god, the judgement you suffer as a parent."

I look at Jude, and see understanding there. But also some pain.

"Did you find that, too?" I ask. I'd like to know, what she's been through.

"Yes." Her laugh is hollow. "But that's another story."

"I'm all ears."

"Well, maybe you could freshen this up first," she raises her near-empty glass to me, "and I'll tell all."

Jude explains what happened, matter-of-factly and without a trace of self-pity, but I find I'm moved to tears. For her. For all of them.

"Oh," I say when she has finished. "I'm so sorry. Really. I know it's a useless thing to say."

"It's fine," she says. "It's life. Sometimes it's shit."

"I don't think that even begins to cover it."

Her little boy, Daniel, had died when he was five, having contracted meningitis. Jude, I am surprised to discover, was at that time in a job not too dissimilar to mine. She was away at a work conference and her husband – I should say ex-husband – Colin was at his office. It was his mum who went to the hospital with Daniel. Colin's dad picked Jude's daughter, Elisabeth, up from school. By the time Jude had switched her phone on, and picked up the messages, Daniel was in intensive care. She rushed back, not minding that she'd enjoyed three glasses of the wine at the conference reception, and she was in such a state that she didn't see a cyclist pulling out of a junction. She ran into her. The cyclist was not particularly injured, but Jude was breathalysed, subsequently arrested, and taken to a police station. A sympathetic police officer listened to her story and arranged for her to be taken to the hospital, but she was too late to see Daniel. He had died without her.

"But you couldn't have saved him." I don't really believe that is any comfort.

"But I didn't say goodbye to him." The pain on her face was almost tangible. "I wasn't there to hold him, when he was poorly."

"And your husband…?"

"Colin? Oh, he didn't blame me. Or he said he didn't. He was – is – a good Christian, and believes in forgiveness. For some things. Anyway, I had guilt enough for the both of us, believe you me."

"So…"

"It was impossible, Lou. How do you come back from something like that?"

"I have no idea."

"And my work had been an issue between us anyway. I'd managed to snag a great job, better paid than his. But longer hours. He was there with the kids much more than me. And after Daniel… I was a mess. I could hardly function. Work were sympathetic but only for so long, and I ended up being offered redundancy, though I understood there was no choice there, not really. It was a generous package, but I really didn't care. Money had lost its meaning to me. And I thought Colin's parents hated me. I couldn't face the other parents at school, where Elisabeth still went, and I couldn't focus on anybody's pain but my own."

I put my hand on hers. She looked at me with a small

smile. "But here I am now," she said, "trying to atone for my sins."

"You didn't sin!" I say vehemently. "God, I hate that word. You didn't do anything wrong."

"Drink-driving?" she suggests.

"Well... in extreme circumstances. I imagine I would have done exactly the same as you."

"Maybe."

"I would. Anyone would. You were trying to get back to your son."

"I was. But I knew I shouldn't be driving."

I felt angry at the thought of everything Jude had gone through, and imagining what it must be like to lose a child. That poor little boy.

"So you and Colin just grew apart?" I've heard plenty of stories of tragedies and traumas being too much for couples to get through.

"Not exactly. I mean, we had already started to before what happened to Daniel. I do think he struggled with me being the main breadwinner. God, another hateful word."

"Hear, hear." I raise my glass to hers, but I don't want to say too much, or insert my own thoughts in here. Jude needed to tell her story. I wanted to hear it.

"Also, as I said, he is quite religious. His faith helped him through, in a way it couldn't help me. I'd gone along with it at first, gone to church with him, and all that. My own parents were not religious at all, and there was something nice about that sense of belonging. Ironically, that was our downfall. Colin introduced me to a woman from the church, who had also lost a child. In completely different circumstances, but it helped, to have somebody who knew at least part of what I was going through. But then she and I grew close."

"Close?"

"Yes, *that* kind of close. It was a surprise to me. But also, a revelation of sorts. It all came to a head when Colin saw us kissing. It never really progressed much beyond that, physically – we didn't really know what we were doing. And I didn't ever think I loved her. But it had awoken something in me. Colin seemed as much concerned about the religious aspect as anything. What would the vicar say? What would the other parishioners think? Anyway, she had cold feet. Went back to her husband, and confessed her sins."

There it is again – that word: sin. "And you?"

"I realised that, while she may not have been right for me, neither was Colin. And word got out, as it was bound to do, and Elisabeth was livid with me. And here we are today. She's grown up, and learned to think for herself, and she no longer minds that I like women. But god, there is so much fucked-up stuff back there, that she can't really make peace with her relationship with me. I get it. I wasn't there for her when her brother died. I was a criminal as well – I was charged with drink-driving, but given the circumstances I was handed a lenient sentence, just community service. Still, Elisabeth hated me for a while. I'm sure I'd have been the same if I was her."

We sit for a while in quiet contemplation. I hadn't expected all this. I don't want Jude to think I am undermining her story, but I do want to get us somewhere more positive. "Do you have any pictures of Daniel?"

"Of course."

"And Elisabeth?"

"Yes, her too! She even came to visit me in the summer. It's a very delicate and fragile thing, our relationship."

"Show me," I say gently, and I squeeze her hand before she withdraws it and rummages in her bag. She produces a small wallet, which has faded photos of a smiling little brown-haired boy, one with an older sister who is missing her two front teeth. There is another photo, of a young woman maybe just a little older than Ada. She is standing with the sea in the background, looking at the camera a little shyly, holding an enamel mug of something hot and steaming.

"They are beautiful," I say.

"Thank you," she says. "For saying that, and for listening."

I don't know what to say, so I put my arm around her, and pull her to me. We hold each other, and then Jude turns to me, her eyes on mine, and before I know it, she is kissing me.

2021

The plan was for Elise to walk up to Tregynon late in the afternoon, to meet Louisa and AJ for pre-dinner drinks. Louisa had told Elise that she had work to do, and wouldn't be able to see her until their dinner appointment. Really, she was just buying some time. Licking her wounds.

At four o'clock, Elise, who was just getting herself ready to go out – unsure how she should dress and look to make her daughter proud of her – heard her phone go. She went downstairs to answer her landline, only for the call to ring off and her mobile to begin buzzing. Her mobile was, of course, upstairs.

"Bugger it!" She hauled herself back up the stairs, to see her daughter's name on the screen.

"He isn't coming, Mum," Louisa said, as soon as Elise answered. She had spent the day immersed in work, trying to right herself. She and AJ had exchanged a few emails, but all to do with the upcoming presentation. It was as though nothing had ever happened between them. He was cool and professional, and she was beginning to think he was not the man she thought he was. Worse, that she had imagined the whole thing.

"Oh, love."

"It's fine," Louisa said tightly. "Just one of those things."

"But everything's… alright… between you?"

"It's fine," she snapped, but was immediately contrite. "Sorry, Mum, yes everything's fine. But I think maybe… maybe I've been a bit too keen with him. He said he had to stay in London, but I could tell something wasn't right.

I asked him, outright. Did he actually want to come down in the first place?"

"And what did he say?"

"He said yes, and then he said no. Well, he dithered, which was annoying, to be honest. I don't have time for ditherers. Said he felt like it was a bit much, too soon. Coming down to Cornwall, coming out for a meal with you. Even though I tried to tell him what you're like. That it wouldn't be some kind of formal, meet-the-parents thing. Just that I think you two would like each other."

"Really?"

"Yes, really, Mum." Louisa sighed fondly. "I know I'm not very good at showing it but I'm proud of you, and I wanted him to meet you and see, see where I'm from. I mean, he's involved in the Saltings, and he's going to be managing community engagement, and I thought it would be good for him to meet you from that perspective, too. Somebody who's lived here nearly all their life but has a good, balanced view of things. Not hysterical, like lots of folk round here."

"Well, thank you, Louisa, for saying that. I really do appreciate it. But I'm so sorry he's not coming. I was looking forward to meeting him. I even had some blusher on."

This made Louisa laugh.

"Yeah, well, maybe it will happen another time. I don't know, though, Mum. I feel like it's gone off the boil. You know when you just know? I think I've been kidding myself. Making it seem like it was meant to be – what with his links to this place. And the fact that he's not a dick – sorry – at work, to me or any of the other women, or lesser mortals. He's always friendly to the doorman,

the cleaners, the guys that deliver the bottles of water...
and he's pretty good-looking too, which always helps."

"Maybe it's not dead in the water yet, love."

"Maybe. But I think I know. If I'm honest, I pushed it,
this trip down here, and him coming down this week. I
should have read the signs, but I ignored them. I think I
just wanted this to happen. Maybe I'm going soft in my
old age. But I think I'd like a relationship. A proper
relationship."

"I suppose, if it's made you realise that, then maybe it's
not been a waste altogether. Perhaps he's not the right
one for you but if you want a 'right one' I'm sure he's out
there. Perhaps AJ's just the catalyst for you keeping an
eye out."

"Maybe," Louisa laughed. "He's too young for me
anyway!"

"Rubbish. If men can do it, women can too. Anyway,
we can still have our dinner, can't we? And pre-dinner
drinks."

"We can. Of course we can. I'd like that, Mum."

They met as arranged, in the hotel bar, which Elise
remembered as the library – where once she had
received lessons, and then a few years later where she
had delivered lessons to her three young charges.

Louisa was sitting at the bar itself, on one of those high
stools. Small and neat, with glossy black hair, from
behind it would be hard to guess her age. When she
turned, as though she had somehow sensed her mother's
arrival, her years were more apparent.

"Mum," she smiled and raised a glass – meant for Elise.
A martini, with an olive on a stick. She smiled warmly,

finally feeling the full weight of Elise's worth, and kissed her mother's cheek. They walked together to a table in the window.

"How are you, my love?" Elise asked as they took their seats.

"I'm fine, Mum. Honestly."

"I'm glad." Elise raised her glass to her daughter's, then took a sip of her drink. "I'd better make this last. I'm not used to cocktails. Just the odd small glass of wine, or cider."

"Well, I wanted to treat you, Mum. And to the meal tonight."

"Thank you, that's lovely of you."

They sat companionably for a while, each lost in their own thoughts. But Elise had something on her mind. Brought to the surface by Louisa's relationship with AJ.

"Lou... You asked, you know, about your dad."

"Yes. I did."

"Do you still want to know? What he was like?"

"Yes, I do."

"Well, OK, then. I'm going to tell you. And I wonder if you already know some of this..." At this moment, their waitress arrived, to take them to their dining table. "I'll tell you in a minute," Elise said, in a stage whisper, induced by the martini.

"OK." Louisa smiled and took her mum's arm. They walked together behind the waitress. "But you don't have to, Mum. Not if you don't want to."

"No. It's fine. I want to. I suppose it needs telling, before I..."

"Don't, Mum," Louisa looked quickly at her, eyes shining. "Don't say it."

"Alright, love. Alright." Elise was slightly stunned by her daughter's strength of feeling.

They took their seats in the dining room, thanking the waitress, and picking up their menus. "Let's order first, Mum. Then we can talk. If you want to."

When their orders were taken and Louisa had selected some white wine, which had been brought to the table and she'd tasted and proclaimed delicious, Elise began again.

"Alright, Louisa. Back to your dad. Davey." She pauses, her eyes focused on a point over Louisa's shoulder, as if she could see right into the past. "He was a good-looking man. Best-looking boy in town, they used to say, and they were right."

Louisa smiled slightly unsurely.

"We met when I was at work, with Maudie, at Fawcett's. When everybody left from the school, well except for Angela, I stayed on here. You know I worked up here as a governess, at first, but then I came back to town and met Maudie, and I met Davey. Who was Maudie's boyfriend at the time."

"He wasn't!" Louisa's eyes shone at this juicy piece of gossip.

"He was. But not for long. And she was soon with Fred, which was the right choice for her. Davey asked me out, and I said yes. A bad move in a little town like this, and I wasn't very popular for a while, I can tell you. Some upstart from the private girls' school, coming and stealing one of their men. Of course, it wasn't like that. I wasn't an upstart, and I wasn't stealing anybody. If anyone was stealing something, it was Davey."

"What do you mean, Mum? What did he steal?"

"Do you mean…? No, it wasn't like that. Not really. I suppose I mean it in a less literal sense. At first, he was everything I thought I wanted. A boy, my age, good-looking and popular, or so I thought. And he had a well-paying job at his family's business. He wasn't always very happy, and I thought I could change that. I wanted to, to make him happy. Sometimes, he was lovely. But, he liked a drink." Elise looked at her glass. "And he had a temper."

"Oh. Oh, Mum," Louisa said. Of course, she already knew some of this, courtesy of Laurie, but somehow it didn't feel right to let on. She wanted to let Elise have a chance to tell her story.

"It wasn't that he was always nasty; not at first. But he did like to tell me what to do. And you know me. I don't really like being told what to do. Back then, though, I let it all happen to me. It felt like everything was always decided for me. Even going to Whiteleys; that was Mum's choice, not mine, though I know why she did it. Moving to Cornwall – decided by the school and maybe local government, I don't really know. After school, Angela found me the job here and said I could live with her. It was incredibly kind of her but again, I had no real alternative option. It's like I was on a conveyor belt, just being carried along through my own life. Then I was with Davey – which ironically was about the only choice I'd really made myself – and ended up pregnant, with Laurie, who else? And then we were married, but by then I don't think we liked each other much at all."

"I'm so sorry, Mum. I didn't realise it happened like that. Although, I shouldn't be surprised," Louisa exclaimed, her outrage driven by her dad's behaviour but also, if she was honest, partially by AJ, too. "And I suppose you couldn't go it alone. Not then."

"Not then, indeed, and if I'm honest, I wouldn't have wanted to. I wouldn't have known where to start. I couldn't even remember my own dad, but he had died, so Mum was a respectable widow. I couldn't be a single mother, it was viewed very differently then. I was stuck. Trapped, really. But I never for one minute resented being pregnant. That only ever seemed a good thing."

"And Dad...?"

"He was reliable, in that he brought home the money. I was never sure how much, because a lot of it also went on drink, but there was still more than enough left over. And of course, we had the house, from his family, and we didn't have to worry about rent, or a mortgage."

"Was he pleased you were pregnant?"

"I suppose he was, in his way. But he wasn't very interested. He was glad Laurie was a boy, I remember that."

Despite everything, the thought that her dad might not have been so excited about her made Louisa's face fall. "So, when I was born...?"

"When you were born, Louisa, and he held you, he was like a different person. I don't think I'd ever seen so much love on his face. But he was an unhappy man, and there was nothing any of us could have done to change that. I think his dad was unhappy before him, and I know he could be very hard on Davey. Seems like that got passed on, and I was on the receiving end. But you need to know that no matter how he behaved to me, he never did anything like that to you or Laurie."

"Did he... hit you, Mum?" Louisa asked, in a hushed tone, across the table. She knew Laurie had said this had happened, but she needed to hear it from her mum. Outside, a boat was heading towards land, coming into the harbour. Elise watched it for a moment. And then the waitress arrived with their food. But the question remained between them and once the waitress had gone, Elise answered.

"He did, my girl, I'm sorry to say."

"Once… or more than once?"

"More often than I can remember."

"When we were there?"

"Sometimes."

"I don't remember."

"I'm glad. Does Laurie?"

"I… don't know. I've never asked him." This wasn't exactly true, but Louisa felt that it was up to Laurie if he wanted to have this conversation with their mum.

"But he doesn't like to talk about his dad?"

"No."

Tears were pricking Louisa's eyes, mirrored in her mum's.

"Louisa," Elise said, "you can ask me any questions you like. And it doesn't have to be tonight. If you want to talk more, we can, but we could also just enjoy our meal, if you'd prefer. I am not intending to shuffle off this mortal coil any time soon, and I promise I'll answer your questions honestly."

"OK, Mum." She thought for a moment. "I do want to ask this, and then maybe you're right, we should try to just enjoy our meal, and being together. But it's a hard question to ask."

Elise looked straight at her daughter. "You want to know if your dad killed himself?"

"Yes. I do."

"I can promise you, my beautiful girl, that he didn't. That is one thing of which I can be sure."

"Really?" Relief flooded through Louisa. What a strange jumble of emotions she had when it came to her dad. Underpinning all of them, despite everything, was love. He was her dad. And Elise had shown some sympathy and understanding for the way he was.

"Really."

"I did have one more thing," Louisa said, twisting her napkin in her hands.

"Ask away."

"Can I come home with you tonight? Stay with you, till I go back to London?"

"Louisa!" Elise exclaimed. "You can come back home any time you like. Any time."

Louisa

As my wonderful mother knows, Jude's kiss is not the first I have received from a woman. I told her all, that evening after the Eden Project. I told her about Gianni, and how I'd been too proud to tell her that I had become pregnant not by design but by accident.

"A happy accident, though," she had said, and of course I agreed. She had tutted about Gianni, but I knew she wouldn't say a lot. I still miss him, in a way, all these years later. I miss the way that he made me feel when I was with him. Nobody has come close to that – not even AJ.

And Mum was unshocked, as I had known she would be, when I told her what had happened, and how it ultimately led to my downfall at work.

When I look back now to my teenage years, and the time Marian said I was going to be like my mother, and my extreme reaction against such a suggestion, I could kick myself. What possible better person could I model myself on?

"So that's why you left work?" Mum had asked me, after listening thoughtfully to the whole sorry story.

"Yes."

"But that's so unfair!" Her first reaction. Anger.

Indignation. "If you'd been a man, I bet things would have been very different."

"I don't know about that."

"Oh come on, Lou, you know as well as I do, these things happen all the time. Men having affairs with their secretaries or PAs, or other more junior colleagues. They don't get forced out."

"I know. I think, though, given the circumstances, I had little choice. But it's alright," I reassured her. "Really. It was the catalyst for me moving back here. Being able to see you. Taking a more relaxed approach to life."

"Well, I can't deny that's a good thing," she smiled. Then she laughed: "I can't believe I thought Tony was your AJ!"

"I can completely believe it. I'm sure I'd have thought the same. It made some kind of sense."

"It makes things a bit easier, with you and Maggie, that he's not."

"There is nothing difficult at all about me and Maggie. I like her, a lot. I just felt a little jealous, Mum, of your friendship with her."

"Oh, my love, as if you ever have anything to be jealous of. You're my girl. You'll always be my girl."

She must have felt a bit torn, thinking that her new friend was going out with my ex. Tony Jones – Anthony Jones, or so she'd thought – but I think Tony is and always has been just Tony.

Mum was sitting on her usual chair, with her view of the street. I had gone to her then, and bent down to hug her. She'd pulled me in closer, murmuring, "My girl," and despite the fact that anyone passing by could see, I'd knelt on the floor, leaning my head against her, and feeling her arms around me, and the incredible strength of this small, elderly woman I am so proud to call my mum.

2021

It was humiliating, going into the office on Monday morning. Even though almost nobody at work knew of her relationship with AJ, Louisa was painfully aware of it. And she did not like feeling humiliated. She had woken that morning with a feeling of dread in her stomach, but even then, and on the tube, and the walk to the office across gum-pocked pavements, she had no idea of the level of genuine humiliation that was heading her way. Not a clue that by the time she put her key in the lock of her front door late that evening, her whole life would have changed irrevocably.

Thank god for Tim, her PA, who greeted her as though he really was pleased to see her. Perhaps he was. Or maybe he was just very good at his job. He knew her, though, and understood just the right level of pleasantries to exchange before updating her on what she had missed workwise while she had been gone – meetings that had been scheduled or rescheduled. Calls that she should return.

At half past nine, she gathered her laptop and a few papers and walked to the lift, travelling up to the conference room on the top floor. The flagship floor, as it was known, where there were a couple of offices and two immaculate, shiny conference rooms with views across the city. Louisa normally enjoyed coming up here, and admiring the sparkling Thames on a sunny day, or the moody clouds moving above the city as autumn drew in. Today, though, her attention was focused on the three people she was meeting initially. One, in particular. AJ.

"Good morning, Louisa," he breezed, as though nothing

had happened.

"Good morning," she replied, calmly and coolly.

"How was Cornwall?"

"It was lovely, thanks," she answered truthfully, thinking that he could have found out for himself.

"Great, great."

She risked a glance at the others. Tony was busy tapping through something on his laptop. Samantha, however, sent a sympathetic glance her way. Urgh. Sympathy. That was not something that Louisa asked for, nor wanted.

"Are we all set, then?" Louisa switched straight into business mode. "What have I missed?"

"We're good to go," Samantha smiled. "With a slight change. Tony is going to present as well. He's been getting a handle on the community engagement aspect."

Which is AJ's job, Louisa thought testily. She was rapidly going off that man. Although she did concede that might be down to bitterness at his rejection of her.

"OK. And I'm...?"

"You'll be fielding questions at the end," AJ cut in. "We thought, as you aren't actually a Canyon employee, maybe it's better for you to take a back seat."

"I... right." He was the client. She had to do what he wanted, although now she really felt snubbed. Her nose painfully out of joint.

So she sat, and she listened to them practise, and offered words of advice or correction when she was allowed to. It felt as though AJ's whole attitude towards her had changed while she was away. She wouldn't admit this to anyone else – well, perhaps John – but it actually hurt.

Samantha seemed to have picked up on something – or maybe AJ had confided in her. Louisa felt the other woman's eyes on her a lot, during the run-through, and during the presentation in the afternoon. The two men (what else?) who ran Canyon had flown in from New York over the weekend. They listened and smiled and nodded while the two young women (again – what else?) who accompanied them took notes and sent emails, while Tim sat next to Louisa, which was some comfort at least.

At the end, Louisa did get a chance to speak, and she knew she did well, but she also knew that the three others had covered it all. Made her feel a bit... redundant, to be honest. So that the Canyon CEO, Gerry, and Abe, the COO, might well be wondering why they had invested so much money in this managed service company when their own company seemed to be managing perfectly well on its own.

Still, Louisa answered the questions put to her strongly and firmly and knowledgeably. This was comfortable ground. She could even offer insight into the location and local community of the Saltings, what with her being a local – "What are the chances of that, huh, AJ?" Gerry asked, and AJ grinned and shrugged.

There followed a dinner, and drinks, and AJ discussed his forthcoming trip to Cornwall, leaving the following day and taking the two New Yorkers with him.

"I've booked us into a lovely little hotel – Trugennon... what's it called, Louisa?"

"Tregynon," she said flatly. She'd had no idea that he was going down to Cornwall this week. Of course, they would want to see the place, and it all made sense, but it still smarted, that he hadn't been there with her, and that he hadn't told her he'd planned this trip, to the same hotel they'd been meant to stay at together.

"Samantha's coming too, aren't you?" AJ smiled at her.

"I am. I can't wait to see it. I wish you could join us, Louisa."

"If I'd known, I would have been glad to." Louisa looked at Gerry and Abe. "I've only just returned from there," she explained. "Visiting my mum."

"Oh, your mom's still there? Maybe we can look in on her."

"I'm sure she'd love to meet you." She sent a hard look at AJ.

The wine was going down a bit too well. She was aware of it, yet she wanted it. Fuelling her anger. Her righteousness. Samantha came back from the bar with a tray of shots. Not Louisa's thing at all, but when one was pushed towards her, and all around the table the others were downing theirs with relish, Louisa found herself following suit. Urgh. She shook her head.

"I know," Samantha said conspiratorially, putting the shot glasses on the tray and signalling to a waiter to take it away. "About you and AJ. How he let you down."

"He told you?"

"Yes, and just so you know, I think he was out of line. I don't think he appreciates you enough, Louisa."

"Well, that's one way of putting it. Thank you, though."

"I mean it. I think you're amazing."

Louisa turned to see Samantha gazing at her. Those eyes of hers were as beautifully made up as ever, thick lashes and eyeliner framing them beguilingly. And her teeth! Louisa vaguely wondered if she should invest in some America-style dentistry. "I don't know about that."

"Oh, you are. I'd like to learn from you."

This was taking a strange turn. But then the whole day had been a bit odd. It was disappointing, after all the work Louisa had done, but she could feel this project slipping away from her. Out of her hands. Canyon had taken her help greedily and now they'd had what they wanted from her, they were moving on. Much like AJ, in fact. Still, she was touched by Samantha's words.

"Well, you know, if we worked for the same company, I would be happy to mentor you. I've done it in the past for a couple of promising young women."

"You'd do that for me?"

"Of course. But... we don't work for the same company. And you live in New York." Louisa laughed slightly uneasily as she felt a hand brush her knee. Or had she imagined it?

Samantha turned her attention then to the CEO, who was asking where the john was. Samantha told him, and as he stood up, his assistant engaged her in conversation. Louisa sat awkwardly, now all but pushed out of the conversations which were going on around her. She risked a glance at AJ, but he seemed to be studiously ignoring her, talking to Abe and Tony. Samantha, however, though facing away, seemed to be sitting so close that Louisa could feel the warmth of her thigh next to hers.

The younger woman turned to glance and smile at her, making Louisa feel a little less left out, and surprisingly grateful. She did not like to feel grateful or beholden to anyone, but she also did not like to feel used up and surplus to requirements. AJ had turned things on with her, only to abruptly press the off switch with no warning whatsoever. And she had been sinking into something comfortable with him. Allowing herself to imagine a future. What an idiot she had been. Well, never again.

"Excuse me," Louisa said, realising as she stood up that she felt quite unsteady. It was strange, because she could hold her wine. It must have been that shot – she should never have done it. Out of character for her, she had allowed peer pressure to determine her decision. Maybe she'd order some coffee on the way back from the Ladies.

"Are you OK?" Samantha asked, her face all concern.

"Yes, I'm fine, thank you."

"Here. I'll come with you." Sammie was on her feet before Louisa could object. She took Louisa's arm – not something Louisa would normally be comfortable with, but it did help her maintain a straight line.

"I think I'll go soon," she slurred.

"Oh no, don't, the party's only just getting started." Samantha looked at her, wide-eyed. As they rounded the corner, towards the toilets, she pulled Louisa to her, backing up against the wall, and before Louisa knew what was happening, Samantha was kissing her.

It utterly floored Louisa. Despite the hand on the knee, and the compliments, it seemed to have come from nowhere, and her brain was a muddle. A mish-mash of AJ, and of this beautiful young woman who was kissing her in a restaurant, her mouth tasting of strawberries and vanilla... at a work event, while their colleagues... boyfriends (or ex, in Louisa's case at least) sat at a table just metres away. And where the CEO of her client company was just coming out of the men's room.

"I—" Louisa pulled away, but not before she'd had a chance to clock Gerry's startled expression. "Excuse me, I've got to…"

She dashed into the ladies' toilet, wondering if Samantha was going to follow her, but for the moment more concerned with making it to one of the cubicles in time. She did, just, and was on her knees, throwing up her dinner, until there was nothing left to come. She retched, wiping her chin, aware that she was utterly alone. Samantha must have returned to the table. And now Louisa would have to do the same.

She looked in the mirror, wiping her running eyes, wondering what on earth she was going to return to. The reality was the worst possible outcome. Finely honed professionals, Gerry and Abe were polite and courteous to her, suggesting they arrange for a cab home. Samantha had slid into a seat next to AJ, and she was looking at her phone. Only Tony was looking at Louisa with any genuine concern.

"I'll get a taxi myself, don't worry," Louisa said, picking up her bag and jacket.

"I'll come with you," said Tony.

"No, no, I'll be fine." But still, he moved next to her, put his hand under her elbow. Walked towards the door with her.

"What happened?" he asked.

"Didn't she say?"

"Who? Samantha? No. But she's been acting strange all day. All weekend, now I come to think of it."

"Has she?" Louisa couldn't really think straight. But she liked Tony. And she was glad he was there with her. Although when he heard she'd been trying it on with his girlfriend – even though she hadn't – he might feel differently about her. She couldn't think any more about that right then, though. She was still feeling decidedly unwell.

"Yes. I think so. She and AJ have been having these quiet little moments, and I feel like I'm busting in on something if I interrupt."

They exited the restaurant onto the busy street.

"Tony, can we talk tomorrow? I'm…"

As a double decker bus passed by, giving all its passengers an excellent view, Louisa bent double and was sick all over the pavement. Some young men in suits, drunk and in high spirits, exclaimed and then walked on, laughing. Louisa's humiliation was complete.

Louisa

Jude pulls away, something like panic, or fear, in her eyes. "I'm so sorry. I shouldn't have done that."

"It's OK," I say gently.

"No, it's not. For one thing, I'm your manager; you're one of my volunteers."

"Well, yes, there is that. But I'm not going to say anything."

I'm surprising myself with how calm I am, and I wonder if this has not come as such a surprise as Jude may have imagined. I take her hands. "You are an incredible person."

She shakes her head, looks down at our hands. "But...?" She looks back at me.

"I don't know. I like you."

"You like me?"

"Yes. I do."

"But you like men."

"I don't know about that!" I laugh. "I can't say I've had very good experiences in that area."

Jude's eyes are on mine, now. Questioning.

"I don't know," I say. "I'm sorry, if I can't be any more definite than that."

"No, no, that's fine."

"I thought you hated me, to be honest, at least at first."

"I didn't…" she laughs and considers her words. "Well, hate is a strong word."

I laugh, too.

"I think you reminded me of me, back then."

"But a million times worse?" I suggest.

"Well, I wouldn't go that far. But I've put that world well behind me now."

"I know you have. And I think I'm in the process of doing the same."

"So…?"

"What I do know is, I like you. I like being with you. I admire you enormously."

"And I didn't completely repel you, just now?"

"Not completely!" I laugh, and squeeze her hand. I think of my grandmother – my mum's mum – and Angela Forbes. The implicit relationship between the two of them. They never had a chance to see what might come of it. "Can we take it slowly? Just see what happens?"

"Yes," she says, "of course."

And now it's my turn to kiss her. But on the cheek, softly, tasting the salt of the tears from her heart-breaking story. And I pull her to me, and hold her, feeling her body gradually relax against mine.

2021

Louisa called in sick to work – something she had done only a handful of times in her whole career. Somehow, illness was not something that had bothered her much. She and Ada too, shrugging off colds and bypassing stomach bugs, even during the nursery and primary-school days. It was a badge of honour to Louisa, although Elise would comment on it as though it were a matter of luck – she too tended to have very few illnesses and ailments, even now that she was older.

"Are you alright, Louisa?" Tim asked, with genuine concern.

Louisa tried to read his tone. What did he know? "No, obviously not!" she snapped at him.

"Yes, sorry. You wouldn't be calling in sick if you were OK!" With a similarly sunny attitude to that of Ada, Tim generally let Louisa's bad moods roll over him. It was another reason that they worked so well together. "How did yesterday go?"

"Yesterday?" she asked sharply.

"Yes, the Canyon presentation. Are they happy with everything?"

"I… think so. Have any of them come in yet? AJ? Tony? Samantha?"

"They're in one of the downstairs meeting rooms, I think. Do you want me to put you through to them?"

"No, no, that's fine." She had expected a call from Samantha, at least. Although, perhaps she herself was embarrassed this morning. Louisa still couldn't quite make sense of it. Was Samantha really keen on her? What about her relationship with Tony? And why was

AJ giving her the cold shoulder?

There was something very odd going on, but she felt extremely fatigued and woolly-minded, and she could not piece it all together. In another near-first, Louisa took her cup of tea back to bed and sank back under the covers – at 8.50am on a Tuesday morning!

Some time later, she was awoken by the clatter of a neighbour filling their recycling bin. The light seeping into the room was fresh and clean, like newly washed sheets. Louisa blinked slowly, feeling decidedly more clear-headed. She padded across the expensive carpet into her en suite and started the shower, watching the mirror steam up. As she wiped the glass and looked herself in the face, something clicked. This was a set-up. The whole thing was a set-up. Of course Samantha wasn't interested in her. Why on earth would she be? They'd set out to ruin her. The question was, why?

She washed herself thoroughly in the shower, shampooing and conditioning her hair twice, as though trying to massage some sense into herself. She stepped across her room, leaving damp footprints as she walked to the huge wardrobe and selected her second-best suit. She had worn her best one yesterday, and look where that had got her.

Phoning for a cab, she switched the coffee machine on for an espresso, then pulled back the skin on a banana, taking a decisive bite. Within minutes, she was on her way.

"Louisa!" Samantha said, shocked at the woman's sudden appearance in the doorway.

"*Sammie*," Louisa said sarcastically.

There were just two of them at the table, laptops open and empty coffee cups nestled companionably together. There was no sign of Tony, nor the Canyon CEO and COO. Maybe they were sleeping off their hangovers.

"I thought you were ill?" AJ asked smoothly. Louisa looked at him coolly, already unable to see what she had previously. Was this really the man she had wanted to introduce to her mother? He was too smooth; too well groomed by far. He and Samantha would make a perfect couple. In fact…

"You two! You're together!" Louisa actually laughed.

Samantha at least had the grace to look a little shame-faced, but AJ just smiled. "Well done. I'm surprised it's taken you this long."

"But Tony…"

"Tony's a sweetheart," Samantha said, slightly uncomfortably.

"So…?"

"Louisa Morgan," AJ said. "It was obvious, when I saw the emails."

"Which emails?"

"Mom had saved them, all these years. Printed off, on a dot matrix. Remember them?" AJ met Louisa's eyes as though she might share his amusement.

"I really don't know what you mean."

Yet… perhaps she was beginning to. She needed him to spell it out, though.

"Here." He took two folded pieces of paper out from his notebook and slid them across to her. Even though Louisa had a good idea what she would see, it still made her mind spin slightly. There, after all these years:

To: LAM_1957@yahoo.com
From: Gcap@hotmail.com
Date: 09/10/2001
Time: 18:56

Counting the days till I'm back in LDN. Gx

Gianni's wife must have accessed his sent items after his death. Louisa could barely think about how painful this discovery would have been for her, against the backdrop of shock and sudden, traumatic bereavement. The second sheet of paper displayed Louisa's email to Gianni:

To: Gcap@hotmail.com
From: LAM_1957@yahoo.com
Date: 11/09/2001
Time: 15:08

I can't believe it! I really hope you are OK and all your friends and family. How utterly shocking. I don't know what else to say. Lxx

"You're his son?" Louisa asked, seeing the sense, but shocked nonetheless.

"Apparently so."

"I had no idea about you."

"Likewise."

"And your mum...?"

"Mom died, two years ago. I found your email then. She'd kept it all that time. Can you imagine? Losing your husband in that act of atrocity and then discovering he'd been cheating on you? She couldn't ask him anything about it. She couldn't shout at him, or even divorce him. And she was loyal. She never told anyone about it. But she kept the emails."

"I'm sorry."

"And yet the damage has been done. It didn't take me too long to work out who you were. This was Dad's company, after all, and good old Louisa Morgan's name is all over the website, the contracts... I knew all about you. But I had to find a way to you. Sammie helped with that, didn't you?"

Samantha was looking down at her hands. She nodded slightly.

"It was just a case of doing our homework, convincing the board that the Saltings was a good foot in the door in the UK, and that we should bring your company on board for a UK base. I knew if we got the Saltings, we'd get you, too. You're from the same shitty little town, for Christ's sake."

"This seems very extreme," Louisa said calmly, while inside her chest her heart was beating ten to the dozen.

"It was an extreme situation. You ruined my mom's life."

"I actually didn't know about her."

"Yet you signed her card. *So very, very sorry.* That was you, wasn't it, Louisa?"

The card. Her small words.

"Yes, it was, but I'd only just discovered he was married..."

"Everyone thought it was plain old grief. If only. He broke her heart. You broke her heart. They'd been together since high school. Had me. Had my sister Jeannie."

"Jeannie."

"Yes, named after Dad. He had quite an ego. And he wanted to lay claim to my sister."

Gianni's face swung sharply into view, to the forefront of Louisa's mind. Those looks they had shared when he strode through the office. That smile. But it was the word 'sister' that had really prodded her brain into action.

AJ smiled, as though he could see the direction her train of thought was going. "She's not my only sister, is she?"

"Oh god..." Louisa sat down heavily, shattered. So AJ was her own daughter's half-brother. And she had slept with him. She couldn't even begin to contemplate quite how messed up this whole situation was.

Samantha actually put her hand on her arm then, as though to comfort her. Louisa pushed it off, fired up by such audacity. "What about you, Samantha? What's your part in this?"

"I just wanted to help," the younger woman said.

"Help who?"

"AJ, of course. He's upset."

"And what was that all about last night?"

"All part of the plan," AJ stepped in. "Your time's up, Louisa Morgan. My mom loved my dad, and you ruined it for her. You love your job, so we're repaying the favour. Gerry and Abe are with your board of directors right now, and I can predict it isn't going to end favourably for you."

Bile rose in Louisa's throat. "This is ridiculous! For one thing, I had no idea your dad was married. He broke my heart too, you know."

"I bleed for you."

"You can't just come in and break up my life like this."

"Looks like I already have." AJ held up his hands as though to say there was nothing more he could do.

"You stay away from Ada."

AJ laughed. "I have every intention of doing so. She's no sister of mine. And don't go thinking she's got any claim to our family money. I've made sure that can't happen. And you told me, there's no father listed on her birth certificate, right?"

She had told him that. When she'd trusted him. When he had seemed like a completely different man to the one sitting in front of her now. It was incredible, how somebody who she had felt so intimate with now seemed like a total stranger.

"Believe you me, I will keep her as far away from you as I possibly can." Louisa turned on her heel and walked out of the room, heading for the lifts. "She doesn't need your 'family money', we've got our own."

A lift pinged, the doors opening painfully slowly. Tony stepped out. "Louisa…" he said, looking concerned.

"Not now." She was fairly sure he was not a part of this, and that he had been used too, but she pushed straight past him, stepping into the lift and pressing the button, letting the doors shut, and feeling herself sink with it as she was carried down to the ground floor. She left the building without looking back, and didn't stop until she had reached her house, where she let herself in, shut the front door, then slid down to the floor, and finally freeing her pent-up tears.

***

The inevitable fall-out came. Louisa was called before her board, and told that her conduct had been incredibly unprofessional, but they thanked her for her service, and offered her a very generous pay-out in return for leaving quietly.

She wanted to laugh. These men sitting in front of her. Geoff on his third marriage. Nigel the confirmed bachelor who had a steady string of young girlfriends, and always reminded her of the Matthew McConaughey line from *Dazed and Confused* – "I get older, they stay the same age." Then there was Brenda, the sole female board member, and the only woman more senior to Louisa. Where she would have liked to find solidarity, she saw distaste and mistrust.

This was the arena that Louisa had chosen to work in, though, and she had been ruthless enough in her time. No doubt this was just the world turning as it should. Her turn was always going to come.

"I'll take it, thanks," Louisa said, not wanting to think too hard about what this meant. But she'd had enough. And AJ had unwittingly done her a favour. Even though she had been so badly mistaken about their relationship, those few months of happiness had opened her eyes wider, so that she could see beyond work and late nights sitting at the kitchen counter in the glow of her laptop. Seeking comfort in a large glass of wine or two, or three or four.

Was it a relationship she wanted? Maybe not. What, then? She wasn't sure. But she was determined she would find out.

She would have to come back, of course, to tie up loose ends, and say her goodbyes to the few people worth saying them to, but she walked out of the meeting and went straight down to the ground floor, stepping out onto the street as though walking into a different world, her head held high.

Louisa

As often happens, all of a sudden, Christmas is upon us. Now, with just a scattering of days to go, I don't resent the Christmas music, or the trees and decorations which adorn the shops, restaurants and cafés. There is a projector lighting up one side of the Saltings with images of snowflakes and presents, and reindeer, and Father Christmas on his sleigh. From my window, I can look down on the harbour and the boats, many of which are also decorated for Christmas, and I'm looking forward to New Year's Eve, having such a lofty view of the celebrations, and in particular the fireworks. I know they're not popular with pet owners, and I understand why, but I can't deny they give me a bit of a thrill, and I am hopeful that next year might be one worth heralding with crashes and bangs and flashes of light.

Tomorrow, Ada will be arriving; the day after that, Laurie. I haven't seen my brother in person for about seven years, which is hard to believe, and is also to my shame. I have regularly said I would go and visit him out on his island, but I never have. Instead, I've relied on seeing him in Cornwall, or meeting for lunch when his work occasionally necessitates him coming to London. Dear Laurie, my big brother who I often felt the need to protect. I can still see his awkward, gawky teenage self, self-consciously walking up the path to the school. It squeezed my heart sometimes, the sight of him. I wish I had been more attentive, but there is no going back now. The only thing I can change is the future (which I realise makes me sound like an inspirational poster), and – I might as well finish it with another classic – there is no better time to start than now.

At the sound of the buzzer, I pull on my winter coat, even though it still isn't really all that cold out, and I pull the door to my flat closed. I go down the stairs two at a time, feeling as young as I have in a long while, and I go into the lobby, where Jude and Tamsin await. Both greet me with warm hugs, and Jude and I share a smile.

"Come on, Lou." Tamsin pulls a hip flask from her pocket and winks at me. "I've brought a little seasonal cheer for us all. It's chilly out there by the water."

"I may have had the same idea," I grin, revealing the little silver bottle in my top pocket.

"You two!" Jude chides. "Don't let the boss see them."

We go outside, and Tamsin links arms with me, then Jude does the same. I think back to this time last year, when I was almost certainly working late, or perhaps sharing an illicit moment with AJ in one of the meeting rooms. Looking back, all of that seems so hollow, and I feel sorry for the person that I was back then.

The singers are just starting up, *O Little Town of Bethlehem*, and the three of us take our positions either side of them, Jude and I holding buckets to collect monetary donations, and Tamsin directing people to the large boxes where they can leave food, drink, and other items to be added to the food hub's stock.

It is overcast, so there are no stars to admire, and no moonlight to fall romantically on the water. And I would love to tell you that as we stand together in the dark winter night, it begins to snow, but it's ten degrees out. Yet all the carol singers – at their centre, Mark, Matthew and John, who turn out to have wonderful voices – are sportingly dressed in woolly hats and gloves and overcoats.

I cast my eyes around the crowd that has gathered, and I see them – Maggie, Stevie and Lucy, and Mum. She sees me looking and she smiles at me, and when she does, I am almost overcome with a rush of love for her. She looks so small, and so old. But so happy.

When the concert is over, hats and gloves and coats are discarded, and John and Matthew load the donations into the hub van, while Mark leads the way to the King's Arms. Maggie lets us in to the social enterprise office, so that we can lock the financial donations safely away, then she rushes off to collect Tony from the station. "See you in the pub!" she calls.

Jude and Tamsin and I walk along the harbourside, Tamsin chattering away about her forthcoming Christmas with her family. Has she any idea, I wonder, of what has passed between Jude and me? I don't suppose she does, and I don't suppose it matters either way. Yet as we reach the end of the harbourside, she looks at us both and smiles, then makes an excuse to run on ahead.

We can hear the noise from the pub before we turn the corner, and then as we do, I can see people are spilling onto the streets with their drinks, even sitting at the outside tables, it's such a warm night.

Jude and I have not spoken since Tamsin went on ahead, but it doesn't feel awkward. Quite the opposite. We walk quietly and contemplatively, for my part at least considering the past year, which has been full of surprises. I find myself taking Jude's hand as we walk, and she jumps slightly, then I feel her fingers curl around mine. As we reach the pub, I squeeze her hand before letting go, then I open the door, and stand back slightly.

"After you," I say, and she smiles at me before walking into the crowded, noisy, cheer-filled pub. I follow close behind, letting the door swing gently shut behind us.

Acknowledgements

Louisa is my fifteenth novel. When I was working on my first book, *Writing the Town Read*, I had no idea if I would even finish it, and certainly not that I would go on to write so many more. It's sometimes hard finding the time to write, and people occasionally tell me they don't know how I do it, but I do it because I want to. I love it.

I had certainly not expected to receive such lovely feedback from readers (some of whom have become friends), and I had also not anticipated building such a great team of people who help me get my books out into the world. I owe thanks as always to my brilliant friend and cover designer Catherine Clarke, who I feel I barely need to give any instructions to these days! She just knows. And Hilary Kerr, for proofreading and offering very helpful insight into the book, its structure, and contents – even fact-checking a couple of details I had missed when I was making some changes! But before the books get to this point, there is my 'beta-reading' team, who are so kind and generous in offering their time, support and feedback. A huge thank you to Marilynn Wrigley and Nelly Harper – both authors themselves – as well as Mandy Chowney-Andrews, Jean Crowe, Amanda Tudor, Kate Jenkins, Ginnie Ebbrell, Tracey Shaw, Sandra Francis, Rebecca Leech, Alison Lassey and Rosalyn Osborn. As ever, I am fearful I've missed somebody out of this list and if I have, I offer my very sincere apologies! All of your help, time and support are hugely valued.

My dad, Ted Rogers, has often helped me with proofreading my books before publishing, as well as being a brilliant advocate for my writing. I'd like to say a big thank you to him. I hope he won't mind me mentioning it's his eightieth birthday this year, and he's impressively active, physically and mentally. He never appreciates quite how good he is, so I am putting it in print here. I have dedicated this book to him and my two brothers but it feels like I am missing our mum out. I know she would be so glad that we have stayed close, and carried on together without her, and of course we are never really without her.

When I began the Connections series, starting with *Elise*, Covid-19 was an entirely alien concept. It has thrown a little bit of a spanner in the works in terms of my planned storylines! I've already written about it in *Time and Tide*, my ninth Coming Back to Cornwall book, but while I don't want to dwell on Covid in Louisa's story, it is impossible to write about events from 2020 onwards without acknowledging it. I hope that I've managed to slide it into Louisa's story successfully, without too much impact.

Sometimes I feel like a bit of a fraud, writing about Cornwall whilst living in Shropshire, and never having lived in Cornwall at all. I try in my writing to consider what it is actually like to live there, not to just be on holiday for a week or two, and I know that life is not easy for many people. Luckily, there is some crossover, as I live in a rural area, and I have first-hand experience of the pros and cons of life in a small town!

I'm lucky to share my life here with my family: Chris, Laura, Edward, and our two dogs, Ash and Willow. The years seem to pass more quickly as children grow older, so I need to make the most of them – the children and the years! Books are important but people so much more so.

Connections One and Two

What dark secrets could a harmless old lady possibly know? Elise Morgan is nearly ninety years old. She loves her family, the sea, and night-time walks. She hates gossip, and bullies, and being called 'sweet', or treated like she's stupid, or boring (and sometimes like she's deaf), just because she has lived a long time.

Elise was sent to an all-girls' school, which was evacuated to Cornwall in the Second World War. She never left the county. She is an orphan, a mother, a grandmother, and a widow. Since her children moved away and her best friend died, life has seemed increasingly empty.

These days, she spends a lot of time sitting at her window, looking out at the world, as if nothing ever happens, and nothing ever has. To passers-by, she might seem just an old lady, but of course there is no such thing. There was once a time when she lived a lot... and there are things she has never forgotten...

Maggie Cavendish is a single mum to Stevie, who has never known her dad, and that's how Maggie wants it to stay. Coming from a steady, stable family home herself, Maggie's world changed irrevocably when her father died, and she discovered something about him that she has never mentioned to her mum, or her twin sister.

Deemed 'the clever one' at school, expectations were set for Maggie from the outset, but what should have been a blessing often seemed exactly the opposite, particularly pitted against her popular and pretty sister Julia, and their best friend, Stacey. It's a surprise to everyone when Maggie discovers she is pregnant.

After years of living with her mum and her daughter, circumstances force Maggie to make a change, starting afresh in a small town on the coast. As Stevie settles in at school, Maggie finds voluntary work at the local seniors' club, and befriends eighty-something Elise. As other parts of her life begin to click into place – an exciting new job, and possibly a new relationship – she rediscovers her sense of self-esteem, and begins to regret not being more honest: with Elise; with her mum, sister and daughter; and with herself.

The Coming Back to Cornwall series

"Total Escapism"

Also by Katharine E. Smith

Writing the Town Read - Katharine's first novel.

"I seriously couldn't put it down and would recommend it to anyone to doesn't like chick lit, but wants a great story."

Looking Past - a story of motherhood, and growing up without a mother.

"Despite the tough topic the book is full of love, friendships and humour. Katharine Smith cleverly balances emotional storylines with strong characters and witty dialogue, making this a surprisingly happy book to read."

Amongst Friends - a back-to-front tale of friendship and family, set in Bristol.

"An interesting, well written book, set in Bristol which is lovingly described, and with excellent characterisation. Very enjoyable."

Coming Back to Cornwall in audio

The whole Coming Back to Cornwall series is being made into audiobooks so you can now listen to the adventures of Alice, Julie and Sam while you drive, cook, clean, go to sleep… whatever, wherever!

The next books in the series will be available as audiobooks soon!

Printed in Great Britain
by Amazon